Prologue

I AM WHO I AM — Creator of the solar system. From the beginning, humanity inhabited a planet that was disorganized and misdirected. So, life on the planet never developed. Instead, humanity's lack of morality and its hypocrisy, along with people's strong attraction along with its propensity toward evil, their awe in the sight of destruction, and death, with, for some, cruelty being the point.

Every individual and civilization, over time, comes face to face with their expiration date of which there was an accounting maintained in mankind's long history on their first planet, Mars.

Of all the planets in this solar system Venus, Jupiter, Uranus, Neptune, Mercury, were off limits following the big bang and as a result there were three out of the eight that could sustain life.

Humans existed on the planet for a million years before it became, what is now known as, the red planet. Mars died because mankind killed it. But there were advancements, by science, allowing for what was left of the planet to pick up and, basically, move to another.

As the earth boiled and sizzled, Saturn and its moons were deemed habitable by men of science. But, this time, the new planet's inhabitability was different. The new planet's destruction wasn't because of wars. Although they did their damage. This time, however, the destruction was mainly due to toxins and pollution which poisoned the air and water, making mankind's second planet, after about another million years, as equally inhabitable, as planet Mars, even billionaires in their lavish million-dollar bunkers succumbed, and as a result, I relocated everything to planet earth, which had cooled significantly by then. Upon the earth I placed two humans Adam and Eve, who were blinded to their past and born again.

The blue planet was mankind's last hope; there were no other habitable planets in this solar system. With the progression of time, I brought aboard three Executives, Buddha was the first followed by Jesus and, finally, Mohammed. Humanity in their respective religions had multiplied faster than expected. The consensus among the Holy Leaders was to allow for the installation of a system to manage mankind. Its name was to be called: Malefic.

I, Divinely, inspired humanity on earth for countless generations. There were humans, for millions of years, on Mars and Saturn. As Creator, Heaven's Executives were placed in Grace because I delegated mankind's stewardship of each soul, who sought representation akin to their ancestors, and these spiritual leaders, in turn, watched over Malefic who watched over Humanity.

The system was good. There was so much data on each soul that it made my job a whole lot easier because I, for once, got to sit back and look at the big picture while my Executives and Malefic worked their intricate magic with their masses.

I received a report yesterday. It wasn't from the Executives, however, it was from the people who have no representative. It was from a man who was born into the world of Judaism, and they have no Executive, I still deal with them directly. After all, it was written that the Jews were my chosen people, because they recognized me first, and I got too attached to them.

One such man was Samuel Isaac. His case intrigued me. He was tested multiple times. I wondered if a human could withstand the worst of what Malefic was capable of. Today, the subject stood above the grave of his nephew. Sam learned from Malefic that he was not a very good soul. He was never very bad or evil; he was in the normal range where most people lived out their lives.

His life, under Malefic's auspices, was magic gone amuck. Malefic existed from the moment of his conception, another event, which was also carefully planned and controlled, through his entire existence, until the day when he reached his expiration date.

There was a celestial meeting and Malefic's report, which was CCd to the Executives, explained that Malefic managed everything. After the meeting Malefic noted that I ordered that Sam be placed into the good/bad world.

There were three dimensions I could have placed him. There was a very good world, which was allocated to the very few. According to the Executives, this world was never to be confused with the material world because that was reserved, mostly, for gluttons; people who worshiped money. But the Executives warned me that the worst, by far, the data showed were those from the bad-evil world, or just plain evil. It, too, was for very few. It had great strength, however, and impacted all the other worlds; its power had always dominated human history.

This was news to me because before I brought the Executives into Heaven, I was as I said a hands-off Creator, for the most part.

Goodness died on Mars. The attribute rekindled on Saturn, but it did not persevere. People on Mars who were on the good side built that world. But people on the bad side destroyed it. All the while, many of the people, the ones in the middle, just sat back and did absolutely nothing. Malefic can't be called upon. It acted when it acted. That is, if it acted at all. It facilitated the birth and demise of every human. From the presentation of each soul into this world, to the end of each life on their expiration date. Each soul's birth date and expiration date was preset. Malefic and the M-team provided the pathways; the individual decided everything else.

Book 1

Chapter 1.

Dorothy, Sam's mother, and Eric, Sam's father, met at a high school football game. He was a skinny and handsome young man in cuffed jeans and white t-shirt and along with his pale skin he wore a crew cut. He came from the visitors' school. Dorothy grew up and lived near the high school she attended. She was very pretty and popular. She was keen on her presentation. She was outfitted in the fashion style of the day; it was a very feminine matching set; her top and skirt were powder blue with white outlines. She wore her perfectly styled brown hair down to her shoulders; a powder blue ribbon weaved through it.

Malefic's M-workers created the pathway that led to their chance encounter; that's all it took. Eric was, even as a teenager, a womanizer. He considered himself to be the Frank Sinatra of his high school. She had numerous friends. She loved to fix herself up, Grandpa said: "You look like a million bucks," and she curtsied to him.

Dorothy looked like a billion bucks to Eric the night they laid eyes on one another; it was a pairing affecting the future but it never lasted. Sam's data showed that Glenda said to him that she believed the coupling happened in order to produce a great human being; herself.

The chemistry between them was good and when they gave birth to their first offspring they truly were very much in love; sexually. Sam learned the character of the man who had fathered him through gossip between Dorothy and her friends after they divorced. He was known as the golden rod. He swooned her for months. The distance between their homes, 35 miles, meant that they spent a lot of time on the phone together. Ruth and Annie, their mothers, sat close-by their telephone stand to monitor their first child's conversations. Annie heard Eric tell his friend that he got to third base with Dorothy. According to Sam's memory data when Annie heard him say: "Sex and candy," she knew the two love birds were infatuated with one another. They were on the phone for hours during the week and they were together every weekend. After the revealing admission ro his buddy, Eric was "ordered," by Annie, to ask for Dorothy's hand in marriage, which he did.

The couples were engaged for their senior year of high school in their respective towns. He courted her for a year. In the 1950s there were millions of post World War II marriages, and Eric's and Dorothy's ceremony was well attended. The couple were married at the Orthodox Synagogue attended by the Steinberg family. The Steinbergs and Isaacs had come together as one on that day but they were very different. Malefic's report revealed that. The dichotomy between the two families was stark. The Steinbergs were Orthodox. Eric's family were reformed. On Dorothy's side Nanna and Poppa kept kosher, and they didn't work on Saturdays. On Eric's side: Annie and Harry were not observant. They never kept kosher. Dorothy said once that they ate spareribs at their favorite Chinese restaurant every Saturday for lunch. Nanna and Poppa were self-employed, they sold shoes at rural flea markets. That livelihood put Uncle Stu through college. Annie also sold clothing items at the flea markets. Malefic reported the origin of the new clothes that she sold was dubious. Not so with Nana and Poppa, they went to shoe factories in Pennsylvania, where they purchased cases of shoes; mostly, factory seconds, and sold them to rural areas across several counties.

Nevertheless, after they married and honeymooned they settled down. Dorothy was a housewife, and Eric was always a salesman. There were many friends in their lives. Several of Dorothy's girlfriends were also married during that summer and each new couple had an offspring. The Isaac family said hello to Glenda.

The Isaacs settled in a new development of row-homes. There was also a strip mall built directly across from the Isaac home. The shopping center consisted of many stores including a bank, a grocery store, a drug store, and a barber. Dorothy's closest girlfriends, along with their husband and newborn, also lived on the block of identical dwellings.

There was a black and white photo in Sam's data, from back then, and it showed the three together. Eric's eyes were closed pretending to be a crooner as he had his arm around little Glenda who was shirtless and looked rather sad. Dorothy stood by the side, she had a serious expression in the picture; she was pregnant with Lily.

Chapter 2

Malefic had power that destroyed a person's world in an instant. Marriages, romances, friendships met with each M-team's scrutiny and conflict was assessed as people were observed and tested. Data was collected that showed how a person managed to cope with life. All the developments. The good, bad or indifferent. The M-team stayed on it. The data monitored every split second. Every minute of every hour. Every day, M-workers collected an enormous amount of information.

By the time Lily was born the first cracks in the family's facade appeared when Eric stayed out late at night with his buddies. It happened too frequently, Dorothy complained to a girlfriend. Eric's buddies included Dorothy's brother, Stu. He was a young teenager influenced by Eric and the others. They regularly congregated at a pool hall where they competed and wagered with one another. Sam had a memory of being there; each pool player had a cigarette dangling from their mouth and the air was thick with smoke.

Dorothy and Eric never drank alcohol but they were heavy smokers. She smoked through all of her pregnancies. The mother, Dorothy Lynn Steinberg, gave birth to a very good soul when Lily arrived into this world. It was a rarity in the Isaac family tree for such a good soul but with the Steinbergs there was a history. His name was Martin Stienberg, and he was a fighter pilot during World War II and he was based in Guam. The account of his life always started with the fact that Martin was a smart young man. He was selfless, charitive, and he gave his life in defence of his country because one night he never returned from the mission; his plane was shot down; the Department of Defense sent a letter informing the family that he was killed in the line of service to his country; it regretted that no remains were recovered.

The newest Isaac addition, Lily, was welcomed into the world with great joy. She was planned, just like Glenda. Dorothy and Eric doted on both of them. Lily was the softest pedal of the family flower. As the girls grew up Dorothy and her girlfriends swapped clothes. Sometimes, Dorothy dressed them up for synagogue with her parents on Saturday mornings. The family often gathered at their Nanna and Poppa home after the service to eat a brunch which consisted of bagels, cream cheese, lox, and white fish.

The days were simpler then. There was little news and a small amount of entertainment from movies and television. Lily found her first love soon after she started school: books. She had her nose in one everyday. She was a good student and angel that Frank and Pat felt blessed with. The younger sister was dominated by the older sister as they developed in life. Glenda was always the prettiest but Lily was the smartest of the two. The data showed that Lily, on average, read two books a day. The sisters were two years apart and Lily received praise because she excelled at school. Glenda was jealous because her younger sister received all A's on her junior high school report card. Glenda earned only one.

Lily immersed herself into books, she moved on from children's books to young adult when she was in the third grade and by the sixth grade she was reading novels.

The two sisterswith their parents moved through their world with little struggle. Dorothy was content. She led a simple life. She played mahjong with her girlfriends on Tuesday afternoons and she took little Glenda and baby Lily with her. Each mother's first little offspring was there and played together, on the floor, with toys, while the babies were within their mother's reach as they played the nineteenth century game.

Both Glenda and Lily were educated in public school and in Hebrew school, which they attended after school on the weekdays at the JCC, the Jewish Community Center. The girls attended class there from grade one through grade 6. Neither were Bat Mitzvahed; it was not custom during those times.

The girls got along but as they grew up there was a distance which gradually builded between them. One notable event in Lily's young life happened when she was eight and Glenda was ten. Eric had taken the girls to the Farm Show, for the harvest festival. It was a cool autumn night, sweatshirt weather. Both girls grabbed hold of one of their father's hands as they made their way to the arena. Once inside, they looked at farm equipment. They saw chickens in cages. Nearby, cows, sheep, goats, and pigs were segregated in pens. Little chicks caught Lily's eyes. When Eric stopped to talk to a salesman, Glenda and Lily wandered to the little chick's exhibit. There were dozens of tiny, yellow I'mfeathered birds in an empty kiddy pool. Little chicks, as innocent as ladybugs. Lily picked up a chick, held it, looked at it, and caressed it. Glenda picked one up too and she closed her hands around it and squeezed it for a minute. As the seconds ticked by she watched in horror as Glenda held her arms out and opened her hands. The chick was dead. She had smothered it. She suffocated it. She squeezed life out of it. Then, to add to the trauma; she dangled the dead little chick upside down in front of Lily's face, and the younger sister screamed when the older sister tried to put the chick into her sister's sweatshirt pocket.

That night Dorothy and Eric talked to the girls about behavior. They made rules about what they could or could not do and they insisted that Glenda was wrong and she should apologize to her younger sibling, which she did, half heartedly, according to the data.

Up until that night, the Isaac home were comforted by family life. Eric still loved and played pool all the time with his friends but now there was more. The new father loved his little girls and they loved him too. After he tucked each one into bed he stood at the doorway and blew a kiss to each one and they blew one back.

The breadwinner went to bed that night and his naked body was immediately stimulated as his being rested next to the bosom of his unclothed wife. A brush with desire escalated for each of them. Energy was exchanged. Each pleasantly overwhelmed by their sexual desire for one another at a moment which intensified rapidly. Dorothy kept a poor track of her menstrual cycles. Whether it was safe for her to have intercourse or not because Eric told her, on more than one occasion, the last thing he wanted was to have another child. He was so emphatic about it that he had her keep a record because she was responsible to tell him when her ovulation period started and ended. That night, Dorothy thought it was day 17 when it was really day 15. As the intercourse continued, it suddenly flowed through her cognition that she wasn't sure about it. Additional data showed that Dorothy and Eric had a number of differences and each questioned their love for each other. Arguments were more frequent and, once, Eric lost his temper with Dorothy when, in conversation, she talked about how nice it was that her best girlfriend was pregnant. The data suggested that it wasn't that she said it but how she said it; her tranquil tone ignited a huge argument.

But that night, irrevocably, changed the course of the Isaac family. Weeks passed until Dorothy reviewed the ovulation calendar that she kept. She experienced mood swings and was overcome by a nagging sadness. She had high anxiety one day, and Eric received a cold welcome that evening, because earlier she determined, to her dread, that on that night they had spontaneous intercourse, her menstrual calendar crossed her mind and she thought it would be okay. But she was wrong; she was two days off. Dorothy was pregnant again. But this time there was no family bliss and the Dorothy and Eric kept it secret from the girls. It was 1957, and the pregnancy was unwanted. They didn't want to have another child but there were no options; she carried the baby through its term and gave birth.

The pregnancy was not easy; just the thought of being pregnant stressed Dorothy out because Eric was extremely angry over the news. As a result, she smoked more and Eric wasn't home as much. His mind and eyes wandered thereafter. He wasn't at the pool hall with his buddies; he was in another woman's arms. Eric's data showed that he had a flood of thoughts about his wife and his children and his responsibility as a husband and a father; it overwhelmed him. He wanted out of the marriage. He hated responsibility. He felt tied down. He yearned to be free. His release never came until family life became too unbearable. It was because of Sam. He had reached a decade in life. The unwanted child lived for nine months in the womb feeling all the negative vibes from his soon to be parents. After Dorothy delivered Sam, they put their differences aside: "for the sake of the family."

Before that the tiny life inside her body was exposed to a ton of toxins. Not just the tar and nicotine but the toxicity of a marriage cracking, a mother carrying an embryo she didn't want, a father who afforded the family very few resources, and after Sam was born, and after Eric left the family, even less. There was one more Isaac to be born, however. They added to their family, in a good will gesture to each other, when Sam was age five, to stay married.

The couple gave birth to another son, Frank. His birth was planned but the love just wasn't there anymore. Frank cried a lot because Sam instigated it. By the time Sam turned ten the older brother teased the younger every day but Dorothy never intervened. She watched them inner-act and she considered it normal sibling inner-actions.

Frank was a docile child. He made friends and had healthy inner-actions with kids his age. He never made trouble; he was a momma's boy. Dorothy babied him because Eric had left the family. Frank never knew his father. The youngest Isaac was brought up by his stepfather, Arnold, a worker at a kosher poultry plant.

Having Frank was a gesture of reconciliation between Eric and Dorothy. The Rabbi, the Steinbergs, and the Isaac's urged the couple to put their individual needs away and to think of the family, and the children in their care. Frank's first five years happened in an air of mutuality. But by that time Sam had reached age ten and both parents had reached their limit and blamed each other, once again, for everything; especially, Sam.

Dorothy was stuck with Sam and, as a result, she took her anger out on him. The report noted that both physical and emotional abuse were leveled at the youngster as he developed by both the father and the mother.

The report also noted that the boy remained unaware of the unwantedness; it was never visible to him on the surface. Sam learned, gradually, it was a secret that was withheld because he was not ready to know. Malefic's report indicated that Sam had no clue how bitter his existence was to those around him. Little Sam needed attention and sought it frequently. That's because, sometimes, the parents neglect the child's needs. That's because they were sick of him by the time their marriage ended.

There was a lot of fault to go around. The Isaacs, Annie and Harry, believed Dorothy failed as a wife and mother. The Steinberg's felt the fault belonged to Eric. But what no one said was that their relationship went sour after Sam was conceived. A decade passed before Dorothy and Eric were separated and divorced.

Chapter 3

Data was exchanged instantaneously. Impulsivity acted as a very strong tool in Malefic's bag of tricks; the human's propensity to do the wrong thing. To make the wrong choice. Until the day when a lesson was finally learned. The individual made the final decision. It was up to them whether to do good, bad, or nothing. Whether to make moral choices and learn lessons the easy way. Or to choose immorality and, as a consequence, the person must learn his or her lessons the hard way.

After Sam was conceived, I informed the Executives about it because the world wasn't ready for history repeating itself once again. And century after century of humanity on earth it never stopped. No lessons were learned. So, I selected someone to tell the people of the world about Malefic because, frankly, I told the Executives, who were in consultation with me, that it was time. I selected, from my long list of chosen people, couples who conceived an unwanted child. I selected Sam's parents because in addition to not wanting the child they were not getting along. Eric cheated on Dorothy, and they separately prayed that they wanted the other: "to fall down a flight of stairs." They weren't educated beyond high school, and they had no parenting skills.

In the days of black and white television there were three major networks. There was no cable TV, no computers, and no cellphones. There was one show that Sam's mother let him watch: *Laugh-In*. It was a very silly hour of goofy comedy, and whenever he was in a social setting; Sam acted out what he saw on the show; he did it for attention. He was hyper and silly but soon nobody laughed anymore. Sam knew had the good common sense to behave and he calmed down when he went to important places. Sam attended day camp at the Jewish Community Center, JCC.

Which seemed to be a recurring theme in Malefic's report. Sam still struggled with what happened at Tony's. He never understood how it affected his life and relationships with other people. His self-esteem was low, and he was just at the beginning of the end. Malefic highlighted in its report:

There was another side to him, his good side, but he was oblivious to it. As reported, his honesty and trustworthiness never developed properly. He never stole from individuals, only from businesses. He had a *Godfather* complex, everything he did, it was just business, and that made it okay. He also failed to acknowledge his lack of friends because of the sexualized mindset that he developed as a kid. Tony entered his life. He had a huge home. It was the biggest and nicest Sam had ever been in. He never understood, until he did, what he did. He had never been naked and had physical contact with another. He thought he was invited to be friends and to play cards or dominos or something like that. Instead, they played stripped *Uno*. Sam went along with it. Tony demeaned Sam. He commanded Sam after he lost the game to follow him. Tony took him into a bedroom where there was a waterbed. At the time there were no VCRs, or any technology used in the twenty-first century, Tony looked at pictures in a pornographic magazine to get the ideas. Those thoughts turned to Tony's desires. What he held in his heart. What he wanted. The impact on Sam was profound. He never made a real friend after that; it made the sexualized hyper feeling within him, which he despised so much.

He told Sam to pull down his pants and underpants and lay faced down on the bed. Sam did what he was told. It dawned on Sam when he thought of it years later, according to Malefic's report, that Tony was exposed to graphic pornography. As a result, Sam was traumatized, and it stayed with him all his life. So, Sam took that pathway. And Tony had a path too. Each pathway permitted each boy to do whatever. Sam never knew what had become of Tony; he didn't care.

Sam recognized, decades later, that he slowly withdrew from any dignity he may have had left inside of him towards himself. A process that slowly inched its way forward. The very first message, the report stated, that Malefic purposely affected Sam the day it happened, and every day which followed; he had a lesson to learn.

Nobody ever told him not to copy what he saw on *Laugh-In*. To behave himself and to show his goodness instead of crazy antics. No parenting addressed the issue, and, consequently, he went haywire. He thought he was supposed to be silly and goofy. He had no reason to doubt it. Some people, even ones in his family, laughed at him, sometimes. As a kid he was starving for attention. Sam emulated nothing positive; he never connected with anyone. He was either silly, goofy, hyper or sexualized and those behaviors never worked for him. He made no friends, and he started to remain alone.

Sam turned off people quicker than flipping the switch on the wall. Before he was a teenager his interactions with other kids were centered around silly and goofy stunts like leaking the air from the neighbor's tire or sending a pizza to them. Sam sat in his mother's darkened room to watch the pizza delivery and the surprised face when he found out they didn't order one, and the neighbor's expression of anger. The report indicated that he did that once. As he got older, he put aside his mischievousness and brought out his nefariousness. He was, however, morphing into someone who, at least, was less reckless when he was around adults. He was quick with a lie to get what he wanted or to get out of trouble so, he'd escape anything negative. And Malefic saw to it that Sam was successful every time. He avoided trouble, and, in turn, he never got into any. His conduct disorder resulted in no consequences. His lack of contact with authority only emboldened him subconsciously and it never fazed him, he just did it automatically just like putting on his underwear in the morning, there was absolutely no thought put into beforehand. Again, he just did it. Impulsivity to the maximus. All he cared about was money to gamble and marijuana.

Sam's conduct disorder stemmed from childhood. Malefic drew no conclusions except to say that Mr. Isaac only saw goodness when he inner-acted with his grandparents. Some of it rubbed off but it was buried deep inside him. He had goodness in him, but it was placed on hold. He was serious and behaved himself on occasion.

But the traumas were paramount, according to his case file. He faced a barrage of them. Malefic ordered the M-workers to ensure that a high alert was issued, and it changed Sam's disposition. To reach the goal Malefic instructed the M-workers to make a very special evening as traumatic as they could for Sam; it was all downhill after that.

Sam being sexualized left him friendless. He tried, many times, to have a sexual experience with other boys his age but it was blocked by Malefic. As Creator, the decision to curtail Sam's actions stemmed from serious concerns which pertained to his future mental health status which was supposed to dominate his being. Sam was abused growing up. There were two incidents in Malefic's report: 1. At age 5, he was bullied in elementary school and in junior high school. During his childhood and adolescence, he was slapped across the face, which was the only violence he ever faced. Each time it was because of something Sam said. The first memory was that, at the age of 5, Dorothy slapped him hard for saying something she didn't like. The other incidents involved peers who were offended by all of Sam's silly and goofy behavior. Sam always ran away from trouble. His attempts to gain anyone's attention and approval fell flat.

He turned off people quicker than flipping the switch on the wall. Before he was a teenager his interactions with other kids were centered around silly and goofy stunts like leaking the air from the neighbor's tire or having a pizza delivered to them. Sam sat in his mother's darkened room to watch the pizza delivery guy's surprised face when he found out they didn't order one, and the neighbor's ire. As he got older, he put aside his mischievousness and brought out his nefariousness. He was, however, morphing into someone who, at least, was less reckless when he was around adults. He was quick with a lie to get what he wanted or to get out of trouble so, he'd escape anything negative. And Malefic saw to it that Sam was successful every time. He avoided trouble, and, in turn, he never got into any. His conduct disorder resulted in no consequences. His lack of contact with authority only emboldened him subconsciously and it never fazed him, he just did it automatically just like putting on his underwear in the morning, there was absolutely no thought put into beforehand. Again, he just did it. Impulsivity to the maximus. All he cared about was money to gamble and marijuana.

Glenda was the force of evil to him. She hurt Sam. She never wanted him around her and everytime he did she'd throw a fit. She shamed Sam for something he should've gotten help from. As a child Sam acted out. There were four incidents. Both involved Glenda. Both were to shame and humiliate Sam.

Sam had reached the age of ten and his troubles involved his dresser drawer; it was before Glenda left him the envelope with the marijuana inside. Sam had taken a knife and carved words into one of the drawers. It read something like: *This is my chest you can't take it. Leave my chest alone.* As soon as Glenda saw it she told Dorothy. I was whipped with a leather strap that night because my sadistic sister wanted to see me suffer.

The other time was when she caught her brother as he masturbated. He was eleven, and Glenda told Dorothy, and when she found out she told me: "You'll get pimples," and when he did, his oldest sister humiliated him about every zit he ever had. She sang songs about it. She'd laugh out loud. Her love for hate was something Sam never understood.

Glenda and Sam never saw eye to eye. Our dichotomy can best be explained when it came to the day that Dad left the family. My father gave up a lot of things throughout his life, and not just wives and children. He gave up on fatherhood because he never wanted it. He and Ellen never had children even though she was only in her mid-twenties when they were married. Dad died a pauper. After his death she told Sam that Eric was forced to marry Dorothy. My grandmother Annie insisted. She told Eric that he must be married to Dorothy. It was an edict, and she merely passed it on. She was used by Malefic. For whatever reason, Malefic ordered it.

It was nighttime. Dad wanted to see us. It was just weeks after their split. Dorothy said that he wanted to talk to the siblings. She put her foot down, however. She refused to let him come into the house. So, Glenda, Lily and I sat in his car. Frank was too young. Dorothy refused to let him see his father. Glenda sat in the front passenger seat. Lily and I sat in the back. Dad cleared his throat before he delivered his eulogy to the family. He told us that he found somebody else that he loved, and he wanted her. He said that he never wanted to live with Dorothy again. Lily lowered her head into one of her hands; she seemed saddened. Glenda 's expression showed that she felt rejected. She gave him her "how dare you" look. Dad noticed it and I saw that he lowered his head, for half a second, in shame. I think she wanted to shame him because, as she saw it, she was being rejected from her position as the first child. Or some other slight she fancied. I, on the other hand, felt nothing. I wasn't happy about it. But I wasn't saddened either. It never phased me. He was never missed. I never hoped or wished that he came back though. He meant nothing to me.

His conduct disorder stemmed from childhood. Malefic drew no conclusions except to say that Mr. Isaac only saw goodness when he inner-acted with his grandparents. Some of it rubbed off but it was buried deep inside him. He had goodness in him, but it was placed on hold. He was serious and behaved himself on occasion.

But the traumas were paramount, according to his treatment plan in his case file, and he faced a barrage of them. Malefic ordered the M-worker's red alarm; it was the highest level in Malefic's system, and that night Sam's disposition was altered irrevocably. To reach the goal in Sam's treatment plan, Malefic instructed the M-workers to make a very special evening as traumatic as they could for him. That night the trauma centered around his day of transition according to Judaism. The entry in the case file indicated that the Orthodox bar mitzvah along with a catered buffet lunch was successful. Malefic, the M-team, from the M-planners to the M-coordinators down to the M-watchers and M-workers, worked on the big event months to ensure that Sam was given a peek into his good world. That night the trauma centered around his day of transition according to Judaism. Malefic and the M-team, from the M-planners to the M-coordinators down to the M-watchers and M-workers came together for the big event months before to ensure that Sam was given a peek into his good world; his connection to Judaism. Later that night would be a different story.

Sam received one gift for the day; a gym bag with his initials on it. Any money given as a gift went to pay the caterer. That night, however, he experienced one of his strongest traumatic events and it was at his bar mitzvah dance. The normally happy day affected Sam's future socialization. He was never hurt like in a fistfight, but Sam's feelings were often hurt. His relationship with his mother was turbulent throughout her time on the planet. Both mother and son refused to show each other their good sides. There was almost constant conflict. They battled every day, but she did nice things for her oldest son, but he never appreciated any of it because he was becoming mentally ill, therefore, he did not appreciate his mother for carrying out her duty as a Jewish mother to have her son's bar mitzvah. It was on a Saturday morning. For that night Dorothy set up, in his honor, a dance. It was in the finished basement of the synagogue; it was considered the community room. The spacious room was decorated for him by Lily. She put up posters. One was a boy and a girl looking at a dandelion. The black and white, poster read, "Let's Be Friends." Malefic highlighted the analysis of that evening as Malefic's report indicated when "life altering trauma" occurred. Sam's conduct disorder, as well as his sexualized mindset bulldozed over anything that was good that day. The trauma was not to take place during the bar mitzvah ceremony.

Instead, the trauma happened during the dance. Dorothy invited 30 kids. They were the same youngsters from the JCC that he never fit in with. He knew them all, but he was a friend to no one and visa-versa. Dorothy never allowed Sam to invite the kids from the neighborhood; kids that he knew all his life. He played with them every day as he grew up, but because they weren't Jewish, they weren't invited. To make matters worse the DJ hated Sam because of his silly and goofy behavior when he was around him, but he needed the $50.

Sam tried to have a good time, but he was laughed at and humiliated by the same teenagers he never liked. Why they were there Sam never knew but it was all arranged to traumatize him more.

In the 1970s, the popularity of the Broadway show, *Jesus Christ Superstar*, was big. Sam listened to the album before, but why on earth did songs from it play at an Orthodox Jewish synagogue; it embarrassed Dorothy and only added to the trauma that he endured that night. As music from the rock-opera played there was a line dance. Sam was moving through the line in celebration of his big day and one of the kids, a kid he disliked, stuck out his foot and tripped the bar mitzvah boy in the process. Sam fell to the ground, and the kid, along with all his friends, laughed as he faced humiliation; it hit Sam hard. The kids who were invited were never friendly to Sam. His interactions with them resulted only to highlight Sam's stupidity. Once on a teen trip they went to a zoo. Later the group of 15 sat at a long table, Malefic reported to gain attention Sam shook a lot of pepper into his palm and as everybody watched as he ate it. He ran to the restroom and got sick; the kids didn't. Malefic's data showed that each teen, at the table, thought Sam was weird.

Why they were there and not the kids who he played with ever since he was a boy was classified by Malefic. To add insult to injury. A very nice rabbi arrived at the synagogue's basement doors that night only to hear: *Jesus Christ Superstar*. If that wasn't enough none of the boys had a yarmulke on which disturbed the rabbi. Yarmulkes were gathered from a bin, and they wereorn.

The entire night was processed in the uncharted areas of Sam's mind. Years later he learned that that space accounted for 80 percent of the brain.

Sam being sexualized left him friendless. He tried, many times, to have a sexual experience with other boys his age but it was blocked by Malefic. As Creator, the decision to curtail Sam's actions stemmed from serious concerns which pertained to his future mental health status which was supposed to dominate his being. Sam was abused growing up. There were two incidents in Malefic's report: 1. At age 5, he was bullied n elementary school and in junior high school. During his childhood and adolescence, he was slapped across the face, which was the only violence he ever faced. Each time it was because of something Sam said. The first memory was that, at the age of 5, Dorothy slapped him hard for saying something she didn't like. The other incidents involved peers who were offended by all of Sam's silly and goofy behavior. Sam always ran away from trouble. His attempts to gain anyone's attention and approval fell flat.

He quickly prioritized what he wanted. He had sporadic interactions with other kids: because sex and marijuana are the only things he desired. He never realized friendship was about having something in common with each other. Something healthy like running, swimming, ping pong, anything but sex because Sam never understood because he was sexualized.

At the age of ten, Malefic analyzed Sam's relations with animals, both wild and domestic. Malefic pinpointed exactly where he plotted on the scale of goodness and evil. He was right down the middle. Never very good but never just plain evil. Pathways were also critical for his education and occupation. Pathways towards or against morality; his level of goodness and evil.

Malefic taught him lessons the hard way. Throughout Sam's youth, he never realized that he was damaged or that he wasn't well. He never knew for decades until he understood and acknowledged that he was not properly educated or prepared for his future life. He was immoral. He needed direction. He never knew there were rules to follow. He broke rules of life all the time because he had severe conduct disorder but it was never recognized. It was treated however, that's when he began to smoke marijuana everyday. Sam made up his own rules to whatever he engaged in. For example, his moral compass. It was formed by his family. Dorothy and Eric influenced Sam before the age of 10, after that only his Uncle Stu, Dorothy's little brother, influenced him once and it was not for something healthy or good. An edict was issued: "Don't teach him." "Don't interact with him." "Don't intervene." "Don't love him." "Don't tolerate him," "Don't mentor him," and "Don't befriend him."

Malefic issued instructions to the M-planners which trickled down to the M-coordinators, the M-watchers, to the M-workers: "Continue providing pathways for him to carry out all nefarious activities. Interventions are non-restrictive. Deep data required

Malefic's report noted: Sam was very mixed up which was on track towards his future development. He was oblivious to what he was doing; a diagnosis of ASPD, (anti-social personality disorder) cluster B: sociopath awaited him on his eighteenth birthday, however, Malefic's report emphasized that Sam's serious mental illness was to remain a secret to him. "He rarely thought about his actions as a teenager, he never felt guilty, and he never showed any remorse in those days," the report concluded, that period of his life would be left for Sam to figure out later as he aged.

There was no ceiling on the limits of his outrageous behavior; he had the freedom to be a very bad person, although he refused all violence. He rejected violence as a tool in his life; he only tolerated it in the movies. He never gave any thought to violence' he never even considered walking on the path of violence. He rejected it and avoided all confrontation.

The summer before, however, he was busy; it's when he committed his first real impulsive crime. He was fifteen, and he spent the summer with Dad and Ellen in California. He was hired part time in a donut shop. The crime took place at night when he worked alone. Malefic's report noted that Sam was puzzled as to why adults allowed him, at fifteen, to work alone at night. He was employed for less than a month. He quit the job after what happened. The store was robbed at knifepoint he decided before he called the police and the owners to report it. They arrived and he told them how it all happened. He simply stated that a white guy in an orange muscle shirt came in and robbed him. Sam was never searched. The teenage thief hid the money inside his bike's headlight as a precaution. Later, he casually rode his bike home; it never even fazed him. In fact, Malefic's report stated Sam was happy with himself. The next day, he quit. He told the owner that his father told him that he wasn't allowed to work there anymore. He committed the crime on a whim. The idea came to mind. Immediately, without a thought, he did it, and he never lost a second of sleep.

He was protected by Malefic, but he knew nothing of it; he went about his days as if he were carrying a white cane. He never thought about his actions; he just mindlessly continued. Every day his thievery continued; it was as if he punched in at work on a timeclock; it was automatically a given. Sam should've landed in prison, and he should've rotted and died there but Malefic and the M-team had the lad under complete control as they presented him with one pathway after another. Just like at his money stuffing job when Malefic allowed him to go as far as he wanted. The magical force was forced to intervene on Sam's behalf many times and each incident required M-workers' magical interventions. Sam knew nothing of any supernatural force collecting data on him as it watched his soul's actions as he moved up, or if he turned around, or he froze in place along the pathway. Sam always moved forward. If there was an impulse, he fed it somehow. However, he never had an awareness at any time about any of it, as was indicated in his treatment plan and the Malefic report stated that Sam processed the Malefic information, gradually, over his future.

Sam managed to avoid the law enforcement courtesy of Malefic. But the system that managed mankind watched, and encouraged his every move, so he got away with nothing. Malefic kept an account of his actions.

After his high school graduation ceremony, he did not celebrate the good day in the good company of others. Instead, he isolated and smoked weed. He graduated from high school, but he had no plans whatsoever. He moved to California to be with his dad and Ellen. He didn't last long. He got a job, but one day he never showed up because he ran away. He loaded up his car and drove to Las Vegas. He was back in California two days later and he was advised, by his mother, to enter the military. "That's what your Uncle Stu did and look at what a mensch he is," she said.

Sam never faced any trouble with his deficits in morality; it allowed him to go into the military. When he entered the navy his wild path followed him into the service, but he wasn't aware of how broken his moral and common-sense compass were.

He never dismissed matters. He never acknowledged it. However, he did nothing about it because he remained unaware of the tightrope he walked on. He never thought about what he was doing; it's business as usual, and consciously Sam was blinded to any future ramifications for his acts by Malefic.

Chapter 4

Human decision making ran the gamut. People were never forced onto a path, but some wondered how and why they got to where they were. They earned their place in each world that they belonged to: The very good world, the pure evil world or the good/bad World whose inhabitants bounced from one pole to the other. Sometimes, it led to catastrophe in their lives which included death. But occasionally, it led to a better world.

Frank was a timid child. Once, Sam dared him to jump off a short step landing over a lawn chair onto the grass. Sam showed him but Frank just couldn't do it. He had a fearful expression and his legs shook and he just couldn't do it. Sam urged him on. He stood in place for a minute. Jumping was too hard for him physically and emotionally. Frank was very skinny as a teenager and he was very tall. He stood six-feet three inches, a record for the Isaac family. As a boy Frank had healthy inner-actions. He made friends easily. He played in sports like basketball, baseball, and golfing. The young man got along with everybody. He was obedient, trustworthy, and honest. Once, he found a wallet that had no ID in it but it held six dollars in cash. Frank went door to door in the neighborhood asking neighbors if they had lost it. The handsome young man worked at a fast food restaurant as a cashier. Frank never even contemplated stealing, according to the data. Frank was a good boy. As a teenager other kids looked up to him, literally but also as someone to model. Everybody loved Frank, within the family. So did his teachers at school. On his report card he was praised for how nice, kind, and helpful he was to his teachers and his peers.

Pat's beginnings began in the suburbs of the northeastern city of Erie, Pennsylvania. Pat's folks lived in Patriot Park. It was a small township, which housed the area's biggest location where people shopped for groceries. Nearby, the VFW American Legion was just a half a mile away from Pat's childhood home. She had moved back in with her parents. Frank later reported to Sam that her mother was a "sweet blabbermouth." She meant no harm, but she had an almost constant homespun monologue of knowledge. She loved to talk. She rarely listened. She'd talk about anything and everything for as long as she wanted. The patient husband, Pat's father, was a well-respected man. He served full-time as a one-star General, in the *National Guard* for thirty-years. George rarely interrupted Dorothy. He kept himself occupied. He reads newspapers, books, magazines, and cereal boxes. Anything, because Frank thought that it distracted or protected him from her almost constant flow of speech. She was always filled with goodness, however. She wasn't a woman to use cross words or to say something bad about anyone.

In the middle of the twentieth century, the Atwill family moved into their dream suburban home. The young couple with two young children flourished in their new surroundings. It became the most popular house in the suburban neighborhood. Its location was racially and religiously segregated. It sat in the white, Anglo-Saxon section of town. Black folks lived in another jurisdiction. Those of the Jewish persuasion made their homes elsewhere, as well.

Every room, above ground, in Pat's childhood home, was small. Their kitchen, its three-bedrooms and two bathrooms were all cramped. The living and dining rooms had more leg room. It, however, had a large, finished basement and was patronized by many neighbors, relatives and friends on a regular basis. It was due to the family's warm hospitality as well as their social skills, and the presence of a large built-in swimming pool in the backyard. It even had a diving board. The whole thing was a rarity in a northeastern state, especially in the 1950s. Other attractions of the home included a large concrete patio for people to congregate. There were lawn chairs, and two picnic tables nearby, where families ate grilled chicken. Inside there were people who congregated. Their murmured voices were drowned out only by a raucous laugh. Cigarette smoke hung in the air. Cheerful and carefree, they kibitzed while they stood close to an authentic bar-table along with a half dozen barstools.

 The bar was fully stocked. It boasted a sink, and a large collection of alcohol-related memorabilia. Neon-beer signs, a giant statue of a hobo who leaned against a post holding a bottle, and a huge lamp shaped like a whiskey bottle.

"If it's the dead of summer, and a weekend, added to a humid afternoon, then the basement and pool are a blessing," Dorothy said. They all wore either a swimsuit, shorts, t-shirts, flip-flops, sandals or they were barefoot. Men showed off their hairy chests. Most of the adults smoked cigarettes as they nursed bottles of beer, glasses of wine, shots of whiskey and various mixed drinks. Those were the happy days, and the alcohol flowed very freely; it was always a good time. Pat was a very popular child. She was smart and outgoing. She inherited her mother's gift for gab. The grown-ups smiled and laughed at her when she sweetly interrupted their small talk. The youngster's eyes showed that she wanted a sip of their alcoholic drink. The adults were amused as the young girl raised her eyebrows as she brightened her eyes and she sipped from their drinks. She just sipped in her early years, but she had her first real drink by the age of twelve.

As she grew she was an excellent student; her mental acuity, her competitiveness; she was an excellent swimmer and was a fixture on her high school swim team. She drank alcohol as a teenager but her sipping days ended in childhood. She was a very light drinker as she entered college. Before that she attended the community college in their hometown. She received an associate's degree in criminal justice. She planned to earn her master's degree. She dreamt that she worked for the FBI, in their criminal division. She wanted to specialize in forensics. She worked hard and earned top grades. She was well on her way to where she realized her goals and her fantasies. But a momentous event dashed it all. She gave it all up just two days before graduation. She never attended the graduation ceremony. She stopped her graduate school research. Her life shifted away from her dreams.

Now, she was on a different path. She lived another life as a result. Instantly, when it happened, her mind told her that she was done. Her subconscious mind, overseen by Malefic and operated by the M-team, searched her data and her profile for alternatives to her future. She panicked and her panic turned to despair. Her thoughts began to wander. She wanted a drink. In her mind she moved far away from herself, and she flew away like a bird.

That day she never got off the ground, however. She faced life altering consequences. She resigned herself to the consequences of the moment. She changed her plans. She immersed herself in her second favorite area of interest: drinking alcohol.

When she heard the siren, the hair went up on the back of her neck. Pat and two of her girlfriends were arrested. She had only smoked marijuana a couple of times. She told Sam that she never really liked it. There was none found on her when she was frisked but she was arrested, nonetheless. She had been a passenger in a car; the inside of which wreaked from the smell of pot. Each occupant was charged. A campus police officer had pinched the trio quite unexpectedly. He was only on duty for a few minutes, he said. Suddenly, the car whizzed by. He followed it and he noticed that the car's movement became somewhat erratic. He pulled the car over. That moment triggered a major shift for Pat. Life now challenged her, much differently, as she walked on her new path. She was thrown off kilter. Her dreams, hopes, and desires were all dashed forever.

It changed the trajectory of her life. She never sought further education in the field she studied. She never applied for any of the dream positions she aspired to for so long. She was not motivated. She never hung in there. She fought the consequences she found herself in. She never launched a battle for redemption. Instantaneously, she knew her future was unattainable, and it was all because, as her father said, she was in the wrong place at the wrong time. As far as Malefic was concerned, she was in the right place at the right time. The M-watchers and M-workers acted. They facilitated the conflict within her. She was thrown off her course. She never fought for what she wanted. She gave up without a fight.

Pat's entire life was turned upside down by the compliments of the M-workers. She told the campus police officer, before she got in the car, that she never knew that they smoked marijuana, and, later, she admitted that she smoked it with them before. She spent the rest of the day in custody. She was released to her father later. She was fined and placed on probation for a year, which she spent at home. She drank alcohol and sulked over her woes. She hid from herself.

While on probation she moved into an apartment in another town. She attended a vocational school and got a certificate in bartending. She worked in the field there for two years, before she decided she wanted to move back home. Nearer to her mother and father, a comfort that she always acknowledged, she told Frank that she missed how her parents always smiled. That they hugged and kissed each other on the cheek, all the time, especially coming and going.

Pat's marriage to Frank coincided with the retirement of her father. After tireless work for the National Guard all those years, George bought a top-of-the-line motorhome, and along with Dorothy, they roamed the country visiting countless RV parks. They took in the sights, the sounds, and the environment while they socialized with other seniors.

Marrying Pat worked out great for Frank. Pat's family sold their dream home to him and his new bride. The new couple now lived, happily, in the house she grew up in. Frank was into it too. He felt love and closeness when Pat brought him home to meet her mother and father. They played *Uno*. Frank never experienced this type of family connection. But after he experienced it, he sought it out more, and soon, he thrived on it. It was a happy period for him.

Frank earned his bachelor's degree. He was hired by the County to collect property taxes. The family was relatively stable. One day, Pat recalled that when she was a girl, her mother placed a wooden stool in front of the kitchen sink. Little Pattie looked excited as she stood upon it. "Look, Mommy, I can see really good now." As Dorothy pointed to different things to see. One of them was: "the pretty lady in the window."

All was well in the Isaac home, and they flourished. Alcohol never passed Pat's lips when she gave birth to Boris, who was born six months after they married. Boris entered the world on a cold and blustery day. Pat tended to the newborn more than Frank, but that was only in the beginning. Once the little guy learned to walk, he was in constant motion. So, the day he wanted to look out of the kitchen window to see the birds, Pat retrieved the small wooden stool from the garage, which was where it had been stored for decades. Pat told Boris the story of the stool, and he stepped up on it. He was stimulated by it. He stood on his tippy toes to see more. Pat pointed things out to the little guy, just like her mother did when she was his age. Suddenly, she appeared. "Look, it's the pretty woman in the window, now she's an old lady," The mother told her son that she had seen her since she was a girl his age.

Later, when Pat gave birth to Sarah, she did the same thing. It was a happy family until it was fueled by alcohol because once Pat started to drink again, which she did after having Boris, and now Sarah, it was a cancer and it slowly grew within the family unit as a whole.

Chapter 5

M-workers operated in the trenches driving all conflict, and it, instantaneously, generated important data which was channeled back to the M-watchers, who shared with the entire M-team, who channeled reports to Malefic. The data covered the gambit of mankind's behaviors. The good and evil held in thought by most. Or, was the person exceptionally good and that evil played no role in the person's mind. Or, was the person pure evil and goodness never played a role in theirs.

He was known as Stu. Stewart Steinberg was Nanna and Poppa's youngest child. He was spoiled because he was nine years younger than their oldest offspring, Dorothy, who mothered him when he turned five and she was fourteen because their parents made a living on the road five days a week. Eric drove, with his wife by his side, a mid-sized boxed truck which provided them with their livelihood. They went to the same flea markets in different rural towns every week for fifty years. The truck, filled with wooden crates of shoes, operated as their business on wheels which put Stu through college. Stu was the first member of the Steinberg family to go to college. Sam's grandparents had high hopes for their son. He was a mensch. "An ace on the bowling lane," Eric told him after he bowled a score of 298 at the Jewish Community Center. A story appeared in the Jewish Community Review along with a black and white photo of Stu in action as he bowled. Stu never disappointed his parents. A young voice in the Beth Israel choir, the boy led a healthy life before he started to hang out with Frank; his new brother-in-law, when he was seventeen and started smoking cigarettes. At fifty-cents a pack he was hooked

Eric and Dorothy made arrangements for Stu's future. He joined the Army Reserve and received a deferment from active duty service. He moved to State College, to attend Penn State University; it was 1968, and they didn't want their son to go to Viet Nam.

For the first time in his life, however, Stu disappointed his parents. His grades at Penn State were poorer than his parents expected during the first semester. He majored in Business Administration and his grade point average was 3.0 – that was good but Eric and Dorothy knew he could do better

Stu stopped singing in the choir at the synagogue although he returned home for the high holidays. He was full voice seated by his father at synagogue as he sang verses along with the congregation.

The Steinberg son earned a bachelor's degree in business administration. His grade point average upon graduation was 3.5 – which pleased his parents. They were proud of everything he did. He researched which business to pursue a career in. He contemplated applying for a job at Nabisco and Hershey foods with a career in wholesale foods but in the end he chose to make his career in aluminum. He landed an entry-level position as an assistant to a broker with SWS, the leading aluminum brokerage firm in the United States.

Stu married Laura Bateman whose parents Ken and Lorraine welcomed Stu as their son-in-law. But they felt differently about the Steinbergs. Ken was a successful real estate broker in the city and earned ten times what Eric and Dorothy earned. They also heard about Sam Isaac, a nephew of Stu's, who was said to be rambunctious and disruptive. They allowed the boy and his siblings to attend the marriage ceremony as the couple took their vows but only Glenda was old enough to attend the reception which followed. Lily was sixteen by then and she drove the boys home.

Stu relocated for his job. The new couple resided in Pennsylvania for a few years and he was transferred to Georgia. After five years of marriage and two daughters, Betsy and Trishia, the marriage ended. Laura kept custody of the girls and remarried. Stu transferred again. This time he was assigned to Fort Worth, Texas.

Stu was skeptical about Texas. At first he thought that there were no Jewish souls in Texas, but he found a synagogue and after he met his second wife, Barbara, a Jewish widow of three impressionable children, all of whom Stu Steinberg placed under his wing and took off like a rocket.

Chapter 6

Malefic was never called upon. It acted when it acted. That is, if it acted at all. It facilitated the birth and demise of every human. From the presentation of each soul into this world, to the end of each life on their expiration date. Each soul's birth date and expiration date was preset. Malefic and the M-team provided the pathways; the individual decided everything else.

Lily was very popular as a teenager. She was always going somewhere, or was doing something. She never wasted her time. Before the age of ten, she was quiet and reserved. After her tenth birthday she was on the swimming team. Sam watched her races. She also volunteered to work at the library. She put books back in their proper places on the shelf. But mostly she sat and talked with the adult librarians. She later recounted that they enjoyed having her around. She babysat a lot too.

A lot more than Glenda, who only did it when it was for rich people who paid top dollar. They wanted someone with "my beauty and sophistication," she once told Dorothy. Glenda met and knew many rich people due to her social connections. It included regular excursions to a posh country club. A girlfriend, from a rich family, took her numerous times, in the summer, to "lay by the pool." Glenda laid there all right. She looked great in a swimsuit with her skin bronzed. She looked rich and she acted rich. She worked the circuit like she had been a part of it all her life. She went to parties, weddings and she "shined," according to her, at wedding receptions. She played tennis and golfed. She was eye candy to the golf-pro, she told her friend: "He offered me private lessons."

As an adult Lily was serious and never made decisions lightly. She knew of a sweet young child named Manuel. The young boy had bounced around the foster care system for more than a year. Lily learned of him through a friend, Angelica who attended her pottery school. Lily worked hard to establish the artistic institute. She bought an old grocery store that sat abandoned for years. She cleaned it up and purchased a pottery wheel and an oven.

Yet the plight of the boy and his future nagged at her for months. Her maternal instincts helped her decide to bring him into her life; she adopted him. Her decision did not surprise Sam, who stated that she plunged headlong into raising Manuel. Sam recalled at dinner when he was young, Lily talked about a girl at school who was a foster child. She felt sorry for her, she later told Sam, because her friend never had a real mom and dad. When Lily said that she wanted to be a foster parent one day, Glenda raised an eyebrow and laughed. But now, according to the data, Sam understood; her dedication to a cause was always full blown. And it registered in his mind that she would put as much fervor into raising Manuel as she had placed over the nation's politics and world affairs.

Lily and Manuel lived in a rural setting. There were numerous trees. The new mom became "an expert," about them, according to Manuel. The spacious single-story dwelling was spread out. Behind it was a sizable lake. Lily sold her pottery school for a handsome sum of money and then she became a third-grade teacher at a local elementary school. Manuel attended the same school.

By the time the boy entered the fifth grade he had mood swings. Lily was very concerned. He stole money, was deceitful, and he lied a lot. According to one of his friends, Manuel was likeable but Lily talked to another mother whose kid said that Manuel had a hot temper.

The boy displayed a lack of happiness at times. He manipulated other kids. They thought that he had more power because his mom was a teacher at the school. He ordered them around like he was king of the school. He played with other kids, but he never respected them or their property. If a kid was nice to him, he'd be a nice guy. One day, Manuel stole a boy's lunch money. The accuser insisted that Manuel took it out of his desk when he and the other kids went to the boy's room. Manuel denied it, but the vice-principal vetoed; she accepted none of it; she got wind, sometime before, of Manuel's temper and deceitfulness when Lily had talked to her about it. She searched the boy, and she found the money; it was exactly what the other boy had reported missing.

The vice-principal interrupted Lily's class. She listened, her eyes widened, as the school's second in command whispered into her ear. Manuel was non-compliant. He refused to let her paddle him because he stole another student's money. Lily's face turned sour. The kids in her class saw her roll her eyes. Most kids hushed up. One kid laughed. Lily motioned for the class assistant to take over. As the heavy-set middle-aged woman rose and slowly moved to the front of the room. Lily and the vice-principal exited. Manuel's mother looked worried.

He was paddled that day. Lily gave consent, but she told Sam that her heart sank when it happened. Manuel expressed his displeasure with a scowl on his face as he took the punishment.

The mother and son relationship, it seemed to Sam, never healed from that day. Manuel became worse as he aged. He had temper tantrums before but they were nothing compared to when he hit his teens. He had trouble with law. He burglarized a neighbor's home, and he took cash off a table. The police were contacted; they determined that Manuel was the culprit. He talked his way out of it. But when Lily learned of it, she suspected him right away. He had $40 on him when they went out to dinner the same night, Sam was told. They had stopped at Walmart, and she was surprised because the next thing she knew he bought a video game. She asked him where he got the money. He told me that the money and the video game belonged to another kid, and that he was given the cash, and he was told to buy it for this other kid. Lily asked him who. He told her I can't tell you because he'd get into trouble. He was no longer a suspect in her mind; she knew that he was the thief. Lily was soft. In her delicate female way, she asked Manuel about it. He said that she berated him. That she picked apart every move he made. She never called the police, but she should've. And she should've told the neighbor the truth, but she never did. She never explained why she let Manuel get away with it. Then Sam thought of Malefic, and he saw things much clearer. Lily was blinded by the supernatural power on that day.

When Manuel reached the age of fifteen, Lily put all the pieces of the puzzle together. Angelica did some research. Apparently, she got her hands on a report. It said that Manuel was given up from adoption by a young mother with mental illness. Also, it reported that the boy was in and out of three different foster homes before the age of four. He was at Child Protective Services for two-weeks before Angelica's agency was contacted again. Her agency never helped CPS when they tried to place the boy before, they knew about him, a flier was circulated, but at the time they had no vacancies. It was the next day, however, when Angelica talked with Lily about him. I never hesitated for a second, she told Sam. She went to meet the boy. That's all it took. She was hooked. She told me later that she thought that he knew how to charm and manipulate someone even back at that age.

 The file on Manuel revealed that he was the product of teenage "hanky-panky." His mother was a naive young woman with bipolar disorder; she never knew that she was even pregnant until her water broke. The father was a sixteen-year-old. His name was revealed but CPS never sought charges against him. The young father was categorized as Latino and he had a juvenile crime record.

Manuel's light brown skin was quite a contrast to Lily, who, literally, was lily-white. Look at the walls of their home and it seemed that Lily and Manuel were a very happy mother and son. They went everywhere, and they did everything together. The framed photos captured the pair at *Disneyland*, *Six Flags Magic Mountain*, cruises, the beach, the mountains, and Washington, D.C. Lily loved this country, and so as part of the child's introduction into American society, they spent four-nights in the nation's capitol city. They toured it and the White House. Along with the Washington Monument, the Lincoln Memorial, the Zoo, and to the Smithsonian museums.

As Sam reflected, he recognized that Manuel's real problem was, consequently, a dangerous one, and it brewed in him. There were only little indicators along the way; however, it became very apparent when he reached his mid-teens. The mother and son had their arguments as he grew up, but then they both made up with one another soon after and then everything was good for a while.

Chapter 7

Malefic and the M-team's expertise was manipulating the inner workings of humanity. There were 200,000 souls brought into this world every day and 400,000 who met their expiration date. Each required the assembly and disassembly of Malefic and the person's M-team.

Frank once referred to Boris as a want-to-be philosopher. By the time he reached teenhood the boy wrote down and offered his thoughts on everything. Things like the covid pandemic. He had a very strong and forceful opinion about it. The respiratory infectious disease killed many people across the globe; it hit the U.S. hard too, under President Paul Pliartrum, and Frank was, according to deep data, very sensitive about the leader. Boris loved Plairtrum too but the trouble maker pushed people's buttons whenever he could. Pat came home and said there was a run on toilet paper at Walmart. Boris laughed and said: "It's okay, he wears a diaper, right dad." Frank blew up at him, and the teen ran out of the house. Pat went out looking for him but she couldn't find him. About three hours later he showed up. This youngster's unusual approach to life; the fact he constantly berated others, showed no respect, and lied. "He's a smart-ass punk," Frank once uttered to Sam.

The boy's attitude befuddled Sam. He was the kind of kid, when encountered by an adult, loved to forget, once they laid their eyes on him. It wasn't always that way. As a young child he, Pat and Frank were all very happy. After Sarah was born was when Boris changed. The adolescent became so idiotic, obnoxious and bittersweet. Nanna said that Boris had a chip on his shoulder as big as a log. From his mother and father to the mailman. From his teacher in school to the bus driver. To him, every single one of us sucked. Adults welcomed his departure. Back then he walked around with a permanent scowl on his face. I recalled that on his last birthday, Glenda sent him a gift card for $50. He looked at it and said: "I love that woman." His reality was warped. Deep down, in a deep dark catacomb of his mind was the real person. The rational mind. The senses of the mind which found pleasure in the smell of a flower or the sight of beautiful painting. It was quite the opposite. Boris had one hobby; violent video games, which Frank allowed. But the father of the brat was out maneuvered. Boris continually pushed his buttons. One time, Boris yelled at Frank "I hate life. I hate you. I hate everyone who is alive." Frank lost it and he smacked the boy across the face, which sent him flying across a coffee table, and in the process, he cracked a rib. CPS got involved. Nothing happened, but Frank walked more tenderly around Boris after that.

Frank comforted his daughter, who was, understandably, afraid of her brother. Frank told her that he was brainwashed by the People Party. Sam, when he traveled, saw the skinny young girl with blonde hair. Her eyes were warm. Her hair was genetically handed down through Pat's family. She was down to earth, Pat told a neighbor. Sarah never sought attention like her brother.

Boris was diagnosed with ASPD, when he was eighteen. Before that, growing up, he was in and out of behavioral programs and institutions, one after another but it was too late according to Sam's data. The boy's behavior in the home angered Frank a great deal. He told Sam about the time when he sat across from a MH worker at one of the behavior programs Boris was in. The experience, Frank recalled, reminded him of the time when he gave up a vicious family pet; it was euthanized at the animal shelter.

Things used to be very normal. The father went to work every day as the mother tended the house with a little nip on the side. Before Sarah could walk or talk, Boris grew up and Frank became his Little League coach. Boris wanted to be a pitcher. Frank heaped praise upon him. "The kid," Frank said, "will be a great pitcher." A decade passed and the boy did not become Sandy Kofax. Frank's interests changed. He mostly ignored Boris and Pat, as the 2016 Presidential election heated up. He loved one guy, Pliartrum. "He says it like it is. He's not some fucking politician. I like the guy." He may have started a love affair with candidate Pliartrum, but he was not spared from the angst that Boris generated.

The kid was every parent's nightmare. What every parent dreaded. That they had conceived and brought into this world, a monster. A school shooter. A mass murderer. Someone who horrified and terrorized the community. In the twenty-first century, it wasn't just the community who was affected. Mass media reported the truly horrifying news non stop; and it spread faster than any wildfire; it went across the country and around the world on the internet in seconds.

Boris' problems started in the family. It included genetics, environment, traumatic experiences and upbringing. He was exposed to adult violence, horror and sex, and he handled it extremely poorly. After the boy pestered him, Frank said it was okay if he watched *The Texas Chainsaw Massacre*. It stimulated all the wrong senses in him; his psychosis, which switched on like a light when he sensed there was prey. He learned he gained satisfaction when he watched or participated in something where people suffered; he got off on it.

Before his early institutionalization, it was one explosion after another. M-workers were busy after M-watchers witnessed an aggression by Boris; he punched Sarah in the face because she told Pat she thought Boris was evil, and he overheard it. He didn't do anything at that time. He waited and confronted her. The data showed that he gained pleasure from the memory. He played it repeatedly in his mind because he felt empowered by it. The teenager's violent act led to juvenile court, which cost Frank money. The judge decided the boy must be counseled. The Justice of the Court stated that the youngster had been through enough behavioral programs. Frank spent hundreds of dollars in co-pays for his so-called counseling; it lasted six months. After returning from the last program he smeared his feces on a gift that Pat gave to her for her birthday. Boris outright bullied everyone on a regular basis. It got to the point that Frank placed a padlock on his bedroom door. He sent him to his room often and locked him in; the boy was locked up if there were any incidents. Or when he was not supervised, especially at night. Frank was beside himself with Boris. "Thank God we still have Sarah," the memory data burned into his soul.

Frank was only comforted by Paul Pliartrum and his 2016 Presidential campaign. That's all he talked about. He socialized with his gentile friends. He never had any Jewish friends when he was young because Dorothy moved the kids out to Patriot Park, so Frank never got to go to the JCC like Sam did. All Sam's socialization was with other Jewish kids, and the report indicated, he did not benefit from any of it. While Frank hung out with gentiles and he made lifelong friends.

Frank wanted to put Boris into another program; the waiting list, especially for teenagers, was long. Sam retrospectively analyzed the problem; it seemed the twentieth-century's juvenile delinquents were tamed in comparison to the SMI (seriously mentally ill) teens of the twenty-first century. A healthy chunk of them were like Boris. He loved knives; his was a hunting knife. It was another birthday gift from his Aunt Glenda. She knew that Frank, Pat, and Boris camped out before Sarah was born.

There were signs of mental illness before he became a teenager. Boris wet the bed and he was one of those volatile kids who was bombarded with technology. Violent video games, graphic television and graphic violence on the internet led him to unleash the worst inside of him. Boris courted evil. There were ramifications. The graphic images of violence and sex to a set of immature eyes can change a kid's psyche. A child never correctly processes what they see. What was meant only for mature adults these images disturbed him. It exposed him. It seemed that the troubled youngster set the stage for tragedy. Malefic along with the M-team and the M-workers ensured most children were spared from exposure to adult violence and pornography; the supernatural wonder waited until the individual faced it on a mature level.

Boris was a very sick young man. Frank never stopped his son from his exposure to adult excesses, sex, violence and pornography. "Why," Sam asked him once? He threw up his hands and said: "There's no stopping him." The student of evil accessed and researched everything he shouldn't which was all made possible by twenty-first century technology. The fact was that he lived on the edge of psychosis. He teetered back and forth ever since he was twelve. But he wasn't diagnosed with conduct disorder until later. The delayed diagnosis contributed to what he did. It made him worse. He was a runaway horse. He was, Sam believed, left to fester. Only, the infection got worse.

Boris sat on his video game chair he was gifted to him from Frank and Pat when he was eight. The boy's fingers got a lot of exercise as he played. He had no friends. He never had a healthy normal relationship. He never dated. He never socialized with anyone. When he attended public school, he had no extracurricular activities. He dropped out of high school in the tenth grade. Pat fought him, practically, every day. But he refused to go to school. People distracted him. I remembered Frank once said that his offspring had no connections to anyone except for those who played video games with him online.

Chapter 8

Malefic, sometimes, controlled a person's thoughts and actions, and there was a good reason for it. The blinded soul was redirected by the supernatural system because it was engaged, at that moment, with a protected individual who required M-worker interventions which served a purpose that only Malefic, the Executives, and I knew.

Sam never dismissed these matters but he never acknowledged and thought about them. There was no thought given to anything Sam did; he acted strictly on impulse. And he did nothing about it because he remained unaware of the tightrope he walked on. He never thought about what he was doing; it's business as usual, and consciously Sam was blinded to any future potential ramifications for his acts by Malefic. Every day his thievery went on; it was as if he punched in at work on a timeclock; it was automatically a given. Sam should've landed in prison, and he should've rotted and died there but Malefic and the M-team had him under complete control as they presented him with one pathway after another. In previous part time work when he was just stuffing his pockets with money because Malefic allowed him to get away with it and to go as far as he wanted. The magical force was forced to intervene on Sam's behalf many times and each incident required M-workers' magical interventions. Sam knew nothing of any supernatural force collecting data or helping him to get away with his crimes hundreds of times. From his constant thievery while he was in high school, to his outlandish stunts involving marijuana, The M-team watched his soul's actions while on the pathway: was he headed forward, or backward, or was he frozen in place and going nowhere at all. Sam's mind was always headed forward in those days; it was altered years later and then it became the norm when he became stuck in the moment; it underwent the process of burning the memory deeply into his central nervous system shaping his personality.

Sam's awareness of his criminality of what he did affected him, at any time, about any of it which was indicated in his treatment plan. Malefic's report stated that Sam processed all the information he received from Malefic, gradually, over his future.

A time came when Malefic presented a pathway that was very risky for Sam to walk upon. The consequences were huge, but potential criminal punishment, namely, being caught never entered Sam's mind. He never hesitated because he had his mind set on something he wanted, and in this case, it was *Enodfoefil*. He recruited two co-conspirators and carried out the plan he developed to accomplish his malfeasance. And in this case his impulse was a planned burglary of the drug store he worked at. Malefic coordinated the affair. The conspiracy involved both Sam, Bobby, and Sally, a co-worker at the store. Each M-team of each youth, their M-planners,

M-coordinators, M-watchers, and M-workers belonging to each soul coordinated plans and actions.

One of Sam's co-conspirators was named Bobby, a youngman he knew from high school. Bobby had an older brother, Steve who sold marijuana to Sam. One day, an impulse came into Sam's mind, and Malefic reported: Sam imagined his greatest risk yet. It propelled him into the world of sociopathy. The conduct disorder implementation was just one year from success: He graduated, so to speak, according to Malefic, from his extreme conduct disorder to Sociopath when he reached age 18, because his criminality went on after that age. However, Malefic planned and had the M-team act. It ordered all M-levels to action and a M-team meeting took place.

The teen who never thought about his future followed through with a conspiracy to burglarize his place of employment for one drug: *Enodfoefil*. There were two five-hundred pill count bottles. The very powerful pain killer sat on a shelf where the pharmacist worked. In Sam's history of stupidity, Malefic noted that his first plan failed because he wanted to do it by himself right under the pharmacist's nose. The nefarious teenager postponed it and left the store after he chatted with a coworker. His second plan worked and unfolded like it was supposed to. Not even a hiccup of a mistake occurred. Later, Sam compensated his conspirators, and he "fenced" the stolen drugs the next day. Before that happened, it sat in the trunk of his 1965 Ford, Galaxy 500. Malefic's M-workers' energy levels were overloaded, according to its report. He drove home that day and Malefic's data showed that Sam's emotional stability dropped. That meant he slowly drained and soon, sometime in his future, the report noted, he would be totally empty emotionally. The events of that day, like all of his other crimes, were influenced by others but not by anything good. His only thought, as he drove home afterward, according to M-watchers: *Don Corleon would be proud of me.*

He had no one to meet and nowhere to go so he stopped and ate at a fastfood restaurant. On the night of the crime another impulse came to the forefront of his mind; go to the bowling alley. The trip placed him on a city street. Trees lined on one side, and a large old cemetery was on the other; it gave him no pause. There was a traffic light ahead. He got to the intersection and the green light turned yellow. He pressed the gas pedal slightly and went through the light before it went red. Within seconds he saw a police car in his mirrors; its lights flashed red as if it were a warning to him about his future.

Immediately, he pulled over. Malefic's data in the report showed: He kept very calm. Not a hint of nervousness. He never crumbled. He never felt besieged.

Quickly, one of the officers used his flashlight to examine the backseat. The first officer told the driver that he had been stopped because he ran through the light. Sam told the officer that he thought he had made it. The officer asked for his driver's license. Sam removed his wallet, and he gave the piece of paper to him; it was not a plastic card with his picture on it in those days.

The operating license was just a card made of special paper with his name, age, address, driver's license number, and the card's expiration date.

Without a reason, the officer told Sam to get out of the car. He didn't ask questions. Immediately he exited the vehicle. He never freaked out. His angel's face maintained its innocent ambiance all through the entire incident. He stood there as the officer dropped to his knees, and he shined his flashlight under the car's front seat. Really, Sam never remembered that he had anything under it. But he did. The officer retrieved a small plastic bong; it was empty and dry. The officer rose to his feet, sniffed it and he looked at Sam. The teenager claimed it was not his and he didn't know how it got there."

Malefic's report stated, the policemen had probable cause to search the entire car at that point; it never happened. M-workers were busy blinding the officers. The police confiscated the bong, and one wrote him a ticket because he ran the light. Malefic reported that it was $10. Without a care in the world, Sam got back inside the car and, then, it crossed his mind: *if only they had looked in the trunk.* Malefic noted that Sam thought, years later, he was so grateful because he should've been thrown into the juvenile justice system and then he morphed into adulthood to become just another convict in prison who scribbled every night.

Malefic's deep data indicated that Bobby, the high school kid, who not only helped Sam with obtaining marijuana and helped with his stolen property, needed to solve a problem. Sam had the privilege, and he enjoyed it immensely. According to the data Sam helped someone because for the first time in his life he had the power and influence which solved the problem. Sam used his influence and it helped Bobby's older sister a great deal. When Bobby told Sam the story of his older sister, Sam's antennas went up.

He told Sam his sister's story and how she tried so very hard to get her SAG (Screen Actors Guild) card but failed at every turn. Bobby said that she was so discouraged that she pondered what happened if she just came home. She lived in New York City and to get a SAG card it required that she obtain SAG employment; a *Catch-22*. So, all doors were closed to her. They were shut until Sam learned of it. He had a cousin in New York City, and he directed television commercials. Through his aunt, Sam contacted him. His family member agreed to see Bobby's sister, and he hired her as an actress to be in one of his commercials. Consequently, she got her SAG card. Bobby was more than pleased with Sam.

Sam prioritized what he wanted in his high school years very easily. He interacted with other kids because marijuana and sex were the only things he desired. Befriending someone was a social skill that went undeveloped after Tony that was why he only yearned for sexual encounters. At the height of one High Holiday, Sam left the orthodox temple and walked to the reformed congregation to see if any kids he knew were there. Sam walked from the Orthodox Temple to the Reformed Temple. He decided to sit on the balcony. He searched for his religion at different times in his early life, and on that day, he found some. There wasn't a soul in the balcony section. The service was in session below. He went to the front row, sat down, and picked up a copy of the Old Testament. He opened it and he looked down. The words popped off the page: *Thou shall not lay with a man the way thou lay with a woman.* Immediately, he closed the book, stood up and walked out.

That intervention was *Malefic's* first attempt to straighten Sam out, but it never did. He hobbled his way through high school. Malefic's report stated: Sam's sexual drive required masturbation because he had no physical contact with anyone except the encounter with Tony. There was a footnote: there was an adult woman in her late 20s, who propositioned Sam, when he was sixteen, and they had sex four times over the course of his senior year. He and Bobby drove around one night. Sam drove to a section of town where there were prostitutes. A police car stopped beside the teenager's car and the cop told the boys that the women standing on the corner were all men. They drove on and Sam had an idea. They drove to the adult woman's apartment and Bobby had sex for the first time. Sam came back later after he took Bobby home.

In his sexualized state of mind Sam emitted the wrong vibes, according to Malefic. He had two sexual experiences with his own gender prior to graduating high school. One was a classmate from Jr. High, and one with someone he worked with after school. One time sexual encounters defined Sam's future sexual history which never functioned normally until he understood what happened with Tony and that never occurred until much later in his life.

Malefic's report noted: Sam was a very mixed up soul. He was on track, however, towards his future development. He was oblivious to the conduct disorder; so, a diagnosis of ASPD, cluster B: sociopath awaited him for his eighteenth birthday. However, Malefic's report emphasized that Sam's serious mental illness was not to be totally revealed to him until later in life. "He rarely thought about his actions as a teenager because he never felt guilty, and he never showed any remorse in those days," the report concluded, that period of his life would be left for Sam to figure out later as he aged.

Sam avoided law enforcement, but only because of Malefic. The system that managed mankind watched and encouraged his every move; but, he got away with nothing. Malefic kept an account of everything.

He managed to graduate high school although Sam never applied himself to anything in any area. He rejected learning often; he believed that he knew what he needed to know. He never learned Spanish because he rejected it in high school, when he had the class to learn the language, because he saw no need for it. Geometry, algebra, statistics, chemistry, and others were subjects he just sat through. He never studied or did homework. His grades in those classes upon his graduation were Cs and Ds. If a test was required to graduate high school he, no doubt, failed.

After Sam's high school graduation ceremony, he did not celebrate the day in the company of others. Instead, he isolated and smoked weed. He graduated from high school, but he had no plans, whatsoever, after that. Impulsively, he decided California was the place for him, so he drove 3,000 miles and lived with Eric and Ellen. His father and stepmother were doing fine. They lived on a cul-de-sac in a nice home in the San Fernando valley. Eric obtained his real-estate license and he succeeded at it. Ellen worked as a magazine editor for a Karate magazine in Los Angeles.

Sam didn't last long at his fathers. Psychiatrically he was a mess but he never learned about mental health; thus, it went untreated. Because he functioned normally, sometimes, he was hired for a job at a restaurant. Soon, the day came when he no-showed at work because his untreated mental illness gained strength within him when he decided to run away. He was unprepared for life. Malefic ordered the M-team that nothing be revealed to Sam, so, as to ensure that he processed nothing that happened..

He loaded up his car and drove to Las Vegas the day he ran off. Organized Crime operated casinos those days and they allowed the 18 year old to gamble. He lost all of his money and he was back in California, two days later and he was advised by his mother to enter the military.

Samuel Martin Isaac was not troubled by his deficits in morality because on paper he was clean, and that allowed him to go into the military; what he did never fazed him. When he entered the navy his wild path followed him, but he wasn't aware how broken his moral compass had become because he was not aware of his immorality; he had no morals because he never learned any. In fact, he learned the opposite There was an incident when he was very young that shaped his sense of morality. Sam was six years old and the boy traveled along with his family and they visited their cousins in New York, and both families went to the New York World's Fair. They had a big lunch. As the Isaac household left, Sam recalled that Eric told Dorothy that he never paid for the food. They both looked into each other's eyes, smirked, smiled and shrugged their shoulders. It sent a nefarious message to the boy. And, perhaps, Sam processed years later it was supposed to.

After Sam returned to California he contacted Bobby before he was to go into the navy and he asked his friend in crime to send him another ounce of marijuana. Bobby did so with great ease. It was sent through *UPS*. Sam went off into his future and after he departed California, he had no further contact with Eric and Ellen until he was discharged from the navy, three years later, after he was honorably discharged as a petty officer 3rd class.

He stayed in a hotel at the navy's expense before he was transported to the Basic Training Reception Station. He heard no opposition within himself because there was no opposition in him about what he did in the past; it was another chapter in his long history of stupidity which is the conclusion he reached years later according to Malefic's report: He traveled for a day on a bus and soon he stood in a military formation at a Navy reception station; he had just arrived and he still wore civilian clothes as he exited the Navy transport. He and other youngmen stood at attention in a formation in silence. Within the first few minutes Sam was in trouble. He was still so very clueless about his wild behavior. The moment was an excellent example of the kind of trouble Sam got into but Malefic intervened and rescued him. That moment would have been a major disaster for him. Malefic's report noted Sam, years later, reflected on it: *I should've been caught. Why wasn't I ever caught?* He should have been charged, court martialed and booted out of the Service, and for those crimes he would be sent to the brig and experience a life filled with misery and despair. But none of that happened. Malefic had a reason for saving Sam, but the youngman never knew about it or its reason for rescuing him time and again.

The RDC Petty Officers scorned the recruits mercilessly. Their sharp eyes pierced every new recruit because they were just inches from their faces yelling at them. They stared at the newly enlisted from head to toe. Before the RDC Petty Officer arrived in front of him, suddenly, Sam had an impulse and he reached down and placed his small marijuana pipe which was in his sock; he unzipped the zipper part of his bar-mitzvah gym bag, which was, also, where he put the ounce of marijuana he got through UPS from Bobby that he casually brought along with him. Sam's data showed he was totally mindless. He never thought of any consequences. He never processed any of his outlandishment because he never thought about himself retrospectively. It was only about what he wanted at the moment and it never registered with him that he had immersed himself deeper into the world of ASPD. In Sam's case he would be diagnosed with Cluster B: Sociopath. He brought an ounce of pot with him when he joined the navy and acted like it was a toothbrush in his gym bag. He showed no emotion, no reaction, no nervousness, no sign of worry because, the data showed, he wasn't. A first class RDC Petty Officer was just three enlistees away when suddenly, a Second Class RDC Petty Officer bursted out of the small wooden building in front of the Seaman Recruits. He pointed to Sam and yelled: "Hey You." He ordered Sam to follow him and the recruit stepped out of formation and stood alongside the wooden building in view of the formations. The livid Petty Officer ordered Sam to take off his sneakers and socks. Without hesitation Sam followed his instructions. The RDC shook his head once because he saw nothing, when he thought he had seen something. He told Sam that he thought he saw the newly enlisted seaman as he placed something into his sock. Sam innocently refuted his claim. And when the navy professional found nothing, he stopped; he went no further; it was the end of the search. There was nothing more to do in his mind at that moment.

Malefic's report was similar to the police incident when Sam was pulled over with 500 pills in his trunk. The RDC had probable cause to go further but he didn't. Sam rarely questioned events, and that included this one for many years to come although he always maintained an awareness of the event burned into his being. He never sought answers because he had no questions; he moved on without thought or reflection.

Sam realized, decades later, after reading, comprehending, and processing Lily's writing that he was saved and that it was Malefic but he didn't know why? If it had gone a different way; if the

RDC Petty Officer took Sam's small gym bag, emptied it and opened the zipper; again, Sam's freedom ended right there. His life should've been altered. But the RDC never searched because he was blinded by Malefic. The suspicious RDC Petty Officer instructed Sam to put his socks and sneakers back on and the military man sent him back into formation. The seasoned sailor looked befuddled but he was satisfied.

Eventually, the risk taker was assigned a bed at the reception station barracks. He had another impulse. When no one was nearby he took the ounce and hid it. He opened his new box of *Crest* toothpaste. He took the tube out and he put the ounce inside it. When he walked into the latrine, above the toilets there was a small, opened air shaft. He stood on the toilet seat and placed it inside; it could not be seen when he looked at the air duct from the ground level. He felt, earlier, that it was unwise to take the ounce of pot with him to his new Basic Training unit which he was soon to be assigned to after he went through the entire reception process when he obtained everything from uniforms to vaccines He concluded the marijuana would be okay in the air duct and he left it right where it was until he came back to get it.

Halfway through the navy training he and the other recruits got a pass. While some went to a movie on the base; others shopped for stuff at the PX, which Sam did too. But after that he didn't walk back with his fellow seaman. He went back to those barracks at the reception station to retrieve his marijuana. The barrack he slept in on his first night was full of brand-new recruits. Sam remembered the sun had gone down and the lights in the billet were on. Sam was in uniform when he entered which was a signal of status among brand-new recruits who were still wearing their civilian clothes. Sam tolf them: "Somebody in my unit is fucking with me, and he hid my toothpaste in the air shaft." Sam went into the latrine, some followed, and the man in uniform stood on the toilet seat, and he retrieved the toothpaste box. He dropped it in his plastic shopping bag. He thanked the guys and left. Back at basic training, his toothpaste box lay in the bag from the PX as he opened it for inspection. Immediately, the door guards were satisfied and let Sam through. He took the contraband inside. He had to place it somewhere. Later, he left the building, and he walked around it. He found a small wooden door, which led to an area beneath the building. He opened the door and scooted in. He pulled the little door closed. The ground underneath the building was layered in sand. He had to stoop as he walked to a nearby corner, and he buried the box. He emerged through the small door. He must have gone in and out of that area a dozen or more times over the eight weeks that he was there. Usually, he scooted beneath the building and smoked a little after dinner and nobody ever noticed him.

Malefic had placed the M-team on high alert when Sam entered the navy. The recruit was still carefree. Later in life Sam thought that one of the reasons he was able to get away with having marijuana in basic training was because one day, in the woods, he found a box turtle. He asked the RDC if the unit could make it a mascot; and the Petty Officer agreed. Sam took the turtle back to the building. He took complete charge of the entire project. He alone walked the turtle, which meant he took it outside and he went beneath the building, smoked a little and he and the turtle returned. Sam made sure it had food and water and upon his graduation from basic training the same RDC officer drove him to a wooded area where he released the creature.

Sam feared nothing and Malefic's report offered recent data when the subject's thoughts: *I smoked pot a thousand times. Why was the pungent smell not on me? It should've been in the air of the rooms I occupied. After I was permanently assigned a unit, I lived in the barracks. The odor should've made its way into the hallways from beneath the door of my room but it didn't. Health and welfare checks took place every month in the barracks but nothing ever happened.* He wasn't the only sailor who smoked marijuana so his actions seemed normal to him. In fact, he partied with many of them on numerous nights. He walked into the latrine, he looked in the mirror and stared at his glassy eyes. Many years later he asked: *Why wasn't I ever caught?*

Malefic's report classified it as a profound intervention. Sam's homosexuality must stop because of what happened with Tony. In the service was raped twice, by the same man, within a three-week period. The incidents took place on the base; they were not at sea. The first incident was when the supply petty officer, Thorn, lured Sam into the supply room. Sam had never met the officer or even seen him before. He was a seaman recruit. The guy was a Second Class Petty Officer. Malefic's report indicated that Sam was raped. The incident was not voluntary. Three weeks later, the same man did the same thing again. He saw Sam after work. Sam never saw him. Thorn followed Sam into his barracks; it was worse than the first, according to the report. The next day, he met with the Lieutenant Commander, and he told him, emotionally, he wanted to move from his barracks. He claimed that he could not tell the Commander what had happened. Sam still worked at the unit, but, as far as where he lived, he was moved into a totally different location that day. The report stated that Sam never saw the guy again.

The incidents were never reported because Sam feared trouble because of his attraction to his own gender and SOP if the navy knew he would be discharged dishonorably, with haste.

He returned to the States because Malefic intervened again. Sam was threatened; a fellow seaman, Carnie, defamed Sam for his homosexuality because Sam never helped his friend. He needed Sam to lie and cheat which Sam did once before for him but Sam let the legal paperwork go through. The sailor had committed an offense that was punishable with a fine. The money was removed from the sailor's pay. The first time it happened, Malefic reported that Sam helped him and didn't send the paperwork through and when it wasn't Carnie promised revenge. Sam was unsettled by it. The next day, however, he was notified that Popa was dying, and the Red Cross planned for an early discharge, since Sam's real discharge date was just three months away. He left that afternoon. He flew back to the United States, and he was processed through the system and given his DD214, Honorable Discharge, proof of his military service.

Dorothy picked Sam up at the airport and drove him to see Nana and Popa. When they arrived the gurney with Grandpa's body had just exited the apartment. Dorothy screamed and fell on her knees. Sam watched Dorothy for several seconds; he did not console her. When they went inside, however, Nana was being consoled by Lily. Sam felt emotionally empty.

Sam's Nana and Popa, the Steinberg's, generated goodness. They were never mean, hurtful or cruel. They exuded calm and non-confrontation. The family's cohesion was free of scandal and tragedy, as were the Isaacs. The data showed Sam felt fortunate, in his later years, that his actions never sullied the names of either family.

Malefic's report stated that the intervention closed the chapter on Sam's Popa. But at the same time, a new pathway for him; it laid bare.

Book 2

Chapter 1

Malefic never acted without reason. A lesson always existed; however, it was seldom learned the easy way. Ever since time was, within every century of mankind's existence, Malefic liked to shake things up. To turn everything on its head. Why? Because mankind deserved the chaos. Wars that stemmed from it happened time and again and whenever it occurred civilians wore blinders provided by the M-workers to keep their conscience clear. It was 1930s Nazi Germany all over again.

When Paul Pliartrum became president no one thought he had a chance. He was written off because of his lack of political experience, his sleazy past, and his ties to organized crime which a lot of people knew about but few had the nerve or platform; it was never discussed. Regular people in his clan never talked about it. Pliartrum made himself, his family, and cronies, and some others rich. Not just the tax cuts for billionaires or bitcoins.The media covered it with oversaturated coverage of Pliartrum's constant outrageousness which meant higher viewership so, that made Pliartrum a cash cow. Viewership was up on Pliartrum leaning channels and from online independent news. Malefic reported that Pliartrum had his thugs ensure that the vendors, at his rallies, paid the president a cut of the lucrative market for all kinds of Pliartrum clothing and paraphernalia. His pettiness had no bounds. But loyalty came first to the US leader. He demanded it from everyone around him because the masses, he thought, were already with him. Paul Pliartrum's naughty past meant nothing to throngs of people who flocked to him. In fact, his followers liked and admired him for it. They were fans of his for twelve years of television and they welcomed him into their living room each week to see him and his guests' antics. These same people loved everything about him: his manner; his words, and attitude. And when he campaigned for president, the first time, he was brash, undisciplined, and he stuck it to the man. Who Pliartrum hated and who he liked. When people watched his show, Pliartrum stood on a pedestal to them and there was nothing that he said or did that his followers didn't like. After he became president, however, their dedication and devotion to him soared to a cult following the likes of which Americans hadn't seen since the Moonies.

Good people. Everyday people. Smart people. Stupid people. The ill informed. The simple minded. They tuned in to see him and his raw talent which involved conflict. Verbal, physical; it didn't matter which as long as it occurred. One show had Lucy who hated Kyle because of his constant womanizing and methamphetamine use and they threw things at one another. There was a bitter argument as each showed their sheer hatred for one another? It was raw television and right out in the open and that was entertainment to his viewers; he amused them and they agreed with him all of the time.

When he assumed the presidency of the United States of America for the first time Pliartrum had always been a player in organized crime. He became its leader when he took office as President. His crimes took place before, during, after he was in office, and even more so, when his second administration quickly rooted itself.

With the election of President Pliartrum, the well established CCP, (Country-Club Party) believed the demonic entities in its coalition were under control. Organized Crime and hate groups like the pride boys, neo-Nazis, white christian nationalist, and white supremists joined in on the festival of hate. The forces of evil found solidarity under the banner of the CCP as their vehicle for political advancement.

In Pliartrum's first term as President, he and his hate coalition were inexperienced, inadequate, and inept because nobody knew what they were doing which was lucky for the country. Their competence was no different than a teenager driving, for the first time, the family car. The former president, according to Malefic's report, had a level-ten evil energy rating; the highest.

Thrusted upon the masses these true events of evil hadn't been seen in many generations. Babies born after major wars like World War II, watched in horror when they reached their senior years because they saw the young generation of the 21st century, coming of age. They were ignorant of history, carefree and reckless, and they made the same mistakes people from the previous century made in its early years. Like a dormant volcano these age-old forces of evil slept, for the most part, in mankind's subconsciousness for eight decades over the 20th century, and before that, during America's civil war in the 19th century. The problem was that wars of other centuries don't interest young people. They read in history books about wars that took place a hundred years ago, but they had no concept of war because to a young person they understood that they happened but it would never happen again, especially in America. The peril the people were placed into was all due to one man: Pliartrum..

His criminality, corruption, and tyranny were transparent; he was crooked and evil on a grand scale. Glenda enthusiastically supported him in his first term, the years between his terms, and his second term.

In between terms, when Pliartrum was at his weakest, he was down. The data Malefic supplied about the former and current president, showed that Plairtrum never even raised an eyebrow of the Executive about his so-called Christianity. In 1989, Jesus Christ, classified Paul Pliartrum as a demonic instigator. Not just for womanizing, cocaine smuggling, money laundering, and sex with underage girls. All his crimes were in Malefic's data, there were numerous prosecutors, and they held sway over his many crimes during his first term, the period between his two terms but no one had laid a hand on him. Malefic warned, however, that Pliartrum, in his second term, was more dangerous than the first.

Pliartrum was in between terms and charged with many felonies when Glenda interviewed him at one of his therapeutic retreats. Retreat members paid a two-hundred-thousand-dollar initiation fee to join his club at Mattula in Sarasota, Florida. The way the former president put it: "There are two-ballrooms. In each five-star luxury suite the bathroom has a chandelier, a dust-free chandelier, can you believe it? It has a marble floor, and many other attractions people will thoroughly enjoy. The best meat. The best seafood. The best wine and the best massage spas in the entire world; the entire world. Can you believe it? You can't find anything better, anywhere. It's the greatest spa in the history of spas, and folks, there's a long rich history there; a real long history; I can tell you that. My spas are more popular than the Roman baths were in Julius Caesar's day. People traveled from all over the world just to spend their time at a Pliartrum retreat. We have the world's most fantastic therapeutic services. Did I say that? And, in the State of Oregon, we broke ground on our new psilocybin retreat; what a place it'll be. I guarantee you'll love it."

Each of his retreats had an impressive lobby along with his name splashed across the front of very expensive temporary housing structures. Each property had a gift shop which sold Pliartrum's brand products. They stocked everything from Pliartrum saline nasal spray to Pliartrum's for dry skin. There was Pliartrum ointment for toe-fungus. Pliartrum shaving gel. A Pliartrum hemorrhoidal treatment. Pliartrum aspirin, Pliartrum cough drops, Pliartrum prophylactics, Pliartrum moisturizer, Pliartrum morning after pill, Pliartrum antacid, Pliartrum witch-hazel, and Pliartrum EpsoM-salt.

Many of his health retreats lost money. The president made his real money from corruption, grifting his supporters, and selling everything from Pliartrum Bibles, bitcoins, to digital playing cards with his superhero image; it all brought in a lot of money.

During his first term in office he and his cohorts struggled because they knew nothing about government. They were all about thuggery but he was surrounded by experienced government officials. So, he was checked during his first term because of it and the covid pandemic which, according to the report, was instituted by Malefic because it was time for America and Americans to learn a lesson.

In his second term, however, Pliartrum placed only "yes" people in his cabinet. They were each billionaires as well; loyal men who carried out his orders which were always to enrich him and themselves. The corruption was on a grand scale. Each action taken as president was crooked and self serving, and each had ties to his financial enterprise; it was organized crime.

Pliartrum was a player way back when. He peddled addictive drugs to Americans. Then came a pandemic. There were many deaths; the deadly virus chiefly targeted those from Pliartrum's own political constituency. Its consequences led to the deaths of a million people during his first presidency.

And Glenda was deeply attached to Pliartrum and his agenda. She and PROX NEWS delivered a banquet of misinformation day and night to those viewers filling the air with Pliartrum propaganda. The purpose for the network's lies, Malefic noted, was to prop up the president and his agenda. The television news channel was on in barber shops and beauty parlors; doctor's offices, US military bases across the world, the list was endless.. People watched, trusted, and were influenced by it, day and night, and what they were told was all lies.

Pliartrum's treason actually started when he received a medical deferment and avoided the draft. He received a pass. He manipulated the system, even at his young age, he stuck it to the man and he never served when he received his draft notice. The future commander in chief avoided VietNam. Later, as President on a day of remembrance at a special anniversary ceremony which commemorated the landing at Normandy he showed his true character. As the ceremony continued he turned to one of his general's, pointed at the mass of land where true patriots laid beneath white crosses; men of valor, who protected Americans; even snobs like him. His utterance to his chief of staff, a former military leader who lost his son who paid the ultimate sacrifice that those men were losers and suckers.

But his serious treason started when he shifted and instituted his thuggery; something rarely seen during his first term in Office. The conspiracy was a day for the history books. The leader of organized crime in the United States and President released his anger and hate on the U.S. Capital, when he lost his bid for re-election following his first term. On that day, he released anger, hate, and violence and changed the course of American history because of his selfishness to remain president after a majority of the people voted against him. J6 occurred in Pliartrum's name. At his behest. It started his war against the status quo which he amplified during his second term. Pliartrum held half of the country which translated to conflict in families. Conflict with neighbors. Conflict with old friends. Conflict with strangers. The atmosphere was always belligerent with him and Glenda helped stir the pot. If there were blue skies, Glenda insisted to her viewers there was something wrong; "it's not blue," the anchor would tell them, "It's black because the People's Party made it black and they are an enemy of America and the Country Club Party (CCP). The people's party is full of communist, cowards and heathens. They want to sexualize your children. They are evil and deserve punishment."

Uncle Stu watched Glenda and her network, practically, every minute of every day; he couldn't be prouder of her. He contributed his time and money to Pliartrum's first campaign but after he was defeated the four year span of time that followed his first term were bad days for Uncle Stu. His morale dropped like a led weight because when his guy was defeated and after J6 happened and they received severe backlash from the law Sam's uncle was down, Pliartrum was down; the entire country-club party was down.

Uncle Stu was not born of privilege; he worked very hard establishing his company. But Plairtrum was born of privilege and hoodwinked his followers. Glenda was a perfect example. She was a beautiful and popular socialite, but Sam data showed that he held in his heart that she was ugly inside. Something else that was ugly was Pliartrum. He didn't just bad mouth someone who he thought wronged him, he wanted retribution against any soul that crossed him.

They were experienced thugs. But older Americans saw through him. After all, Sam told Lily: "I saw *The Godfather* fifty-times." Apparently, Pliartrum believed that nobody knew his dirty little secret. The takeover of America by Organized Crime. *Don Corleone*, if reported correctly, turned over in his grave at the news. The mob always wanted to buy judges and politicians, to put them in their little pockets. Now they demanded judgeships and political office themselves. Their thievery had no boundaries. Glenda and Uncle Stu saw people like Sam and Lily as dead meat. On television, one night, a follower at a Pliartrum rally, in a silent second, spoke up and bellowed: "When do I get to use my AR-15 against these bastards?" Pliartrum's crowd hooted, hollered and applauded, enthusiastically.

Bubba did that a lot. He hooted and hollered when it was *J6*. He hooted and hollered Pliartrum's attacks on our institutions, primarily, the Justice Department, the FBI, ATF and other institutions dedicated to catching criminals, like the IRS went after tax cheats. These were the same institutions that organized crime feared in its long history and who wanted vengeance against authority. That same authority that put people like Pliartrum out of business. Before his presidency there were many Federal agencies who fought, every day, to weed out criminals like him and these law breakers were placed into prison. But the rich criminal's acts never faced justice; courtesy of Malefic. It was time; America had a lesson to learn. And the protection Pliartrum received throughout his life was similar to when Malefic tested the German people before World War II as they embraced Hitler and his ideology.

Intolerance prevalent in society increased. On air, she was called the queen of hate. She didn't care and enjoyed dishing out Pliartrum's daily hogwash. Transgender spider's carried diseases. The Missouri River, the longest river in the country, had its name changed to: The Tick Tock River because the mega social media network bribed Pliartrum for a few million dollars and he issued an executive order and changed it.

Glenda trashed the people's party nightly. Her news show had at least one new story that would make the people's party voters outraged and furious. Guest after guest, Glenda discussed nothing but pro-Pliartrum propaganda with them. Her nightly mantra was that the opponents of Pliartrum and the CCP were evil. Every night, she stuck it to the other side. She wanted the establishment and independent news media to report how terrible she was; it was all free press, Glenda the star who had a bank account that rivaled some countries, didn't have enough; she wanted more.

Glenda saw Paul Pliartrum, Jr., the elder's number two son, for the first time at an CCP event that showcased one of Pliartrum's retreats in Pennsylvania. During his first term, billionaires and millionaires drank the finest wine and ate all the best food at the taxpayers' expense, that event cost hundreds of thousands of dollars. That wasn't the worst of it. Pliartrum milked the coffers of this country like a dairy farmer, and the cow was known as Bubba. Pliartrum, his family, and all his real-life, genuine, died in the wool Country Club Party establishment, played Bubba like a fiddler. His fans followed Pied Piper Pliartrum like he was Peter Pan, and they were off to Neverland. The CCP establishment were deathly afraid of Bubba because they were Pliartrum's private army. They called judges and journalists with death treats and harassed them relentlessly. CCP Bubbas showed up at school board meetings with Nazi like agendas. Department stores selling garments which Bubba disapproved of were shamed. CCP Bubbas marched forward with their extreme priorities like banning books and drag queens from public and school libraries. But in Pliartum's first term Bubba was, for the most part, stymied.

When Pliartrum was sworn into office the first time, he placed one hand on the Bible and raised the other as he took the Oath. He swore to protect and defend the Constitution of the United States of America. Malefic's report indicated that Pliartrum's sociopathy overshadowed his thoughts; his impulsivity level was similar to a four year old child, therefore, he was stupid.

Glenda attended the Inauguration and considered herself to be a close confidant to the President. He called her up at any hour and they discussed what was on his mind. Their relationship was so solid Glenda traveled to Washington and, privately, ate lunch with him at the White House on more than one occasion.

Paul, Jr. guested, remotely, on Glenda's show several times during the president's first term; Junior kept coming back because the anchor was: "So hot and so beautiful," according to Dorothy. So, when they met in person, she hit him hard. The former president's number two son left his wife and five children for Glenda. They grabbed the headlines as the "power couple." The press, especially Glenda and PROX NEWS, never got enough of Pliartrum. The reason was as clear as Lake Tahoe; he's been so good for business. Pliartrum made a lot of people a lot of money. Glenda benefited when she had fallen into the good graces of her potential new father-in-law even before she connected with Paul, Jr. The former Commander in Chief characterized her as the voice of reason and blessed Junior's divorce; he welcomed Glenda into the fold, unofficially, because, again, she had limitations on her contract.

"I offered advice which the president took seriously," according to Glenda. She communicated with her mother, Dorothy, every day and Lily was no different. She, too, called her mother each day and updated her on the truth because their mother chose to watch PROX NEWS and Glenda; "she is the biggest star.," Dorothy told a girlfriend. Even though she watched PROX it never meant that she followed and believed everything she heard. She would say: "Whose truth, Pliartrum's!"

The day came when Glenda showed up for a family gathering. Full of politics, Sam's youngest sister, Lily, told Glenda that the president and his people were real organized crime players. "It is so obvious," she said. "Pliartrum and his entourage looks as if they were right of central casting. The media stated, too often, that Pliartrum and his team were just like or similar to organized crime. Established CCP members were afraid because they feared Bubba. CCP established members' reelections held sway but Bubba's dangerousness saturated the party after Pliartrum lost, because the CCP of old feared the former president and Bubba. America had reached its danger zone. CCP regulars were scared for their own lives and the lives of their families. Pliartrum and Bubba controlled every CCP member.

Pliartrum was always a player in the organized crimes of big pharma. He became the leader of it when he took office as President. His crimes took place before, during, and after he was in office. Crimes against the country and humanity. With the election of President Pliartrum, the established Country-Club Party believed that they controlled their coalition which included organized crime and white supremesist; Nazis and Christian Nationalist. The established CCP was blinded by Malefic because it challenged the sanctity; the core value of this nation; its democracy. The CCP of old wanted their party back, but they feared the monster they created. The old timers knew Bubba ate disagreeable party members for Sunday brunch. A great dark cloud inched its way over the Party's Headquarters because M-workers gathered data suggesting that three people's lives intersected and it required the attention of each souls' M-planners.

Pliartrum was down when he lost his bid for reelection. He faced the Law during this period. He had his mugshot taken; he had practiced his evil expression endlessly. He was forced into a courtroom that was too cold. Judges who opposed him were singled out. They and their families were targeted.

Lily followed all the Pliartrum news. She listened to NPR and watched CNN when she wasn't busy at work or doing something with Manuel. Once, late on a Saturday night, Lily watched a Youtube video about the plight of Pliartrum. America's west coast wrapped up its day in an hour, but it was already early morning on the east coast. On occasion Malefic, its M-team, and M-workers used their magical influence and intervened in human affairs.

After the shady president lost the election and he was out of Office, Malefic summoned the leader of each soul involved in an upcoming pivotal moment that required amplification. Each M-team ordered its M-workers who oversaw, Glenda, Lily, and former President Pliartrum. The connection between Glenda and the washed-up leader of the free world was well established. He appeared on her show regularly after he lost. The former president wanted the Pliartrum name on the tip of each American's tongue. Good or bad. He just loved being on top, the person everyone talked about every day, all the time, morning, noon and night. Whether good or bad, he accepted all of the publicity he could get.

The Youtube video Lily watched Saturday night was four minutes long. It appeared on one of Youtube's regular political pundit's channels. The commentator felt that Pliartrum was immune from being imprisoned for his crimes against the Constitution and American people because there was no place to house him if he were to be jailed. Lily commented:

If we need to build one just for them, Pliartrum, his family, and all of his co-conspirators must be prosecuted and imprisoned. The greatest traitors that this country has ever seen, can't go unpunished. Pliartrum's Prison can be built on the hundreds-of-thousand acres of federal land in the Nevada desert. He can slap his name on it just like his other ill-gotten properties but he and the culpable country club must face serious consequences. His secret service can take shifts guarding his cell. As to the country cubbers who stood by to shove these lies down the throats of Amerocicans, you should all be in Pliartrum's prison too. Don't let organized crime rule America! Stop them before it's too late!

Lily called Sam about nine that next morning. He sensed, from her alert tone, something unusual had happened. It appeared to her that Pliartrum responded to a YouTube comment that she wrote the night before. She told Sam that just three hours after Lily left her comment on the video Pliartrum posted on his social media platform:

No President has done more for Israel than I have. Somewhat surprisingly, however, our wonderful Christian Right friends are far more appreciative of this than the people of the Jewish faith, *especially those living in the U.S. Those living in Israel, though, are a different story- Highest approval rating in the World, could easily be P.M.! The U.S.* Jews *have to get their act together and appreciate what they have in Israel - Before it is too late!*

She argued that what they communicated was all in the timing, and the words made it clear to her that he responded to what she wrote. She said the exchange of scribbles on the internet blew her mind. The fact that the former and now current president responded to her comment on Youtube; her, an average citizen, showed that Pliartrum couldn't withstand the barrage of criticism that she threw at him; it hurt, and specifically the overall theme of her organized crime post about the man and what she believed to be the truth. She would have added that the 45th president was a sociopath and that Pliartrum was so seriously mentally ill (SMI) he refused to recognize it because to him he was the most powerful man in the world.

His life's demise was not on his radar screen ever; he believed that he could live forever, basically. So, now, he was outed by Lily. His dirty little secret was that he was leader of organized crime in America, and a one-term president until 2024, when Malefic intervened; it was now because of Pliartrum, America's time to be tested. The supernatural force looked at the state of the United States as critical because the moment was right. All the signs were there that American society needed to suffer, and that was the pathway that the consensus of people wanted.

The younger generations of voters, again, never factored in the early 20th Century; it's like they failed to learn the lessons of WWII; it was like WWII, Hiler and the Nazis never existed, and they, along with the the ignorant people who never took action, and they just let it happen. They never wanted Pliartrum and all of his craziness and they wanted their country-club party back. But now they were afraid of Pliartrum and his thugs. They not only threatened the individual but their family and extended family as well. And it happened because it was too late. Now, Pliartrum was in complete control and he and his organized crime buddies would never relinquish it.

History now belonged to Pliartrum and his followers who loved him with all of their hearts, and the new voting generation of Americans embraced it, just like Germany's youth, as they joined the Nazis and Hitler. These older and younger generations made this all possible, and they are responsible just as much as the older generations of adult people who stood by and said nothing. They never warned the youth from Hitler's day because, once again, history repeated itself and because Malefic reported that America did not learn its lesson from Pliartrum's first term because organized crime was not organized, and that the nation chose a very dangerous and mentally ill man as their leader since Adolf Hitlet.

So, apparently, Youtube video comments that were exceptionally good or bad were downloaded and shared with him if it met those standards. Apparently, Lily met those standards. Also, of course, her name appeared above her comment; it was easy to deduce her Jewish heritage from her last name which he now had and that scared her. She told Sam after she read his post: "I never made the connection to my comment by what he wrote about American Jews. But when I got to his last sentence, which matched mine, the hair went up on the back of my neck."

We talked for an hour. Lily believed Pliartrum became irate over certain sentences and specific words that she put into her comment. She believed she hit him hard from the beginning. Each punch landed and they only became worse as the comment went on until the very end when Lily insisted: *Don't let organized crime rule America. Stop them before it's too late!* She imagined the scene. Pliartrum had his minion of assholes gathered when an aide said: Boss, this comment was left on a Youtube video a few minutes ago. And since the sociopath does not read, the aide read the comment to the stupid leader of America, and she laughed as she pictured the scene as it played out to what she wrote. The aide who read the former president's comment placed it in front of him when he finished. Pliartrum snatched the paper off the million dollar coffee table and said: "Who is this mother fucker," Lily quipped to herself and giggled making it part of her cognitive thought process. She figured that pissed him off even more and thought that if her comment pissed him off enough to respond with a post with a personalized veiled threat at the end, then he'd be pissed off enough to take Lily Isaac's name from the top of the comment and place her on his enemy's list which another aide added to on a daily basis. That morning it was Lily Isaad.

Pliartrum had a very long enemy's list. It included politicians, journalists, actors, and musicians. But it also included many average citizens who opposed him and Lily was now one of them. If she had her way she wanted to be a White House correspondent just for a day. In that period of time there was a scheduled press conference with Pliartrum and the Prime Minister of India, for example and she was chosen to ask the first question, and it was for Pliartrum. Lily would stand strong as she asked: "President Pliartrum, you often refer to the White House Presscorps as fake news. What would you say to the average American who states that you're a fake president? That you are really in charge of organized crime in the United States, and that you're the leader of organized crime in this country operating an organized crime and that you are operating organized crime right out of the Oval Office. That you're not doing the people's business you're doing your business, and it's all about, organized crime. And the person who asked the question responds to your lame answer by saying: ""Don't let organized crime rule America.""""

"What would you say to him in response? Are you a fake president, sir? Has organized crime infiltrated the Federal Government, sir."

Apparently, Pliartrum believed that nobody knew his dirty little secret. The takeover of America by Organized Crime. It was written that *Don Corleone*, turned over in his grave at the news. The mob always wanted to buy judges and politicians, to put them in their little pockets. Now they demanded judgeships, ambassadorships and political office themselves. Their thievery had no boundaries. Glenda and Uncle Stu categorized people like Lily as dead meat. On television, that night, a follower at a Pliartrum rally, in a silent second, bellowed: "When do I get to use my AR-15 on those bastards?" Pliartrum's crowd hooted, hollered and applauded, enthusiastically, their agreement.

Bubba did that a lot. He hooted and hollered when it was *J6*. He hooted and hollered Pliartrum's attacks on our institutions, primarily, the Justice Department, the FBI, ATF and other institutions dedicated to catching criminals, like the IRS. These were the same institutions that organized crime feared and who the Federal government fought, every day, to weed out and to imprison.

Organized crime veterans never imagined, even in their wildest dreams, the leader of organized crime in America being Paul Pliartrum. He was a joke. New York mobsters tolerated the rich boy. They let him into their lives. Pliartrum was just what they were looking for; a front.

Pliartrum was never challenged by anyone in the Country Club Party. Why would they? He did nothing wrong. He gave them tax cuts after all. While in Office and out of Office he took no responsibility for any of his crimes. The guy was a petty crook. He was a b-list celebrity from a washed-up television talk show.

So, Malefic created the conflict and blinded Pliartrum's people from a mountain of truth. If they only knew that they were played the whole time by the master manipulator and bubba was the sucker. Evil flourished under Pliartrum and the Country Club Party's elite stood by and watched and then it happened.

Chapter 2

One of the saddest expiration dates was those who departed at a great age; if murder entered into the equation; it produced a shock to a person's central nervous system.

Found only after she missed church, a 90-year-old woman was savagely murdered in her home. It happened on a quiet residential street in Patriot Park, an area not prone to the kind of savagery the detectives, on scene, found. Detective J.D. Wicks worked for the city. The word came down to him on a day of rest. It was anything but. He searched the victim's home. He inspected his people's work in the garden beds. He saw his fingerprint woman in action, as she dusted the windowsills. He inspected a shed and as he emerged a flock of ducks honked as they flew overhead. He watched them. He admired ducks, and his grimace face mellowed for a second, that is, until he noticed a home nested above the victim's property, 100-yards away. He looked back and forth from one window to the other. Each had a kitchen window that faced each other all that distance away. He thought for a moment and then came the hunch. He walked back inside the house, into the kitchen, and looked out its window above the murderer victim's sink. The football field distance continued because it intrigued him for some reason.

Through the kitchen window Pat saw the police activity in the distance. Yellow tape surrounded the murder house. She saw uniformed police officers and a few plain clothes detectives.

Later, when asked by police she said that she always gazed out the window while she rinsed and washed kitchen ware in the sinks; she liked it. Pat's house was the one that she grew up in but it was Frank's backyard, now. Fenced all around with its built-in swimming pool, concrete decks, and patio; he worked hard to keep it nice. He showed it off to others whenever he got the chance; it was more than he ever cared for or showed off Boris, according to the data. On the opposite side of their backyard, Pat had a view that she had seen all her life, a large wooded area filled with trees that shed their leaves every year. She later told Sam that she had looked over the trees, and down at one house, "Ever since I was tall enough.". In the winter, when the tree branches were bare, she had an even better view. At the kitchen window of the two homes, Pat said that she watched a family who grew up there. She remembered that she saw kids, a grown-up man and woman at their kitchen window ever since she remembered. They each had a bright light above the sink. Pat looked down at the house and its residential street. "I watched a family change." When she thought about it, she said that ten-years ago, she noticed the man and the woman still appeared in the window. That was it. Years passed, and then there was only the woman. She never saw the man anymore. "Just her," Pat said. She never knew who the old woman was who appeared at the kitchen sink. But everybody in Frank's house knew of the woman who, by now, was old, gray, and hunched over. She still hand washed her dishes, Pat said.

As Pat rinsed a coffee cup she listened to a reporter, live, on the television, who was at the scene of the brutal murder. She turned off the water because her eyes expressed that she couldn't believe what her ears heard. Between the reporter's voice and the sight, she witnessed over the trees, down at the old woman's house, she was alarmed. There were emergency and police vehicles with red lights flashing. She saw two men at the kitchen window. She later learned that they were detectives.

When Frank came home from work, he was surprised; his wife, right out in the open, was drinking. Usually, she waited until after dinner before she drove off to the Legion that she worked at on weekends. She went on her days off as well. She drank, smoked and socialized there seven-days a week.

The husband noted, according to Malefic, that his wife had a glass of vodka mixed with orange-juice in her hand that day. She was seated on the sofa. The television volume was off the charts. The couple talked about the old woman and her murder and what she saw outside of the kitchen window.

Frank stepped back from the kitchen window after he saw the police presence and an ugly thought entered his mind but it was trumped when he looked back at his wife.

He was sick of her frequent drinking and smoking; he never smoked cigarettes. It was bad enough that he made her sleep on the sofa, because she reeked too much to lay beside, he said. Pat told Sam that Frank didn't love her anymore. "Her drinking was such that she hid bottles around the house," he said. She told Sam the story about the day she knew that Frank didn't love her anymore. Frank brought her home from the hospital. Her hospitalization was related to her health problems for her addiction to alcohol. Riding home from the hospital she had an accident. She bled through her tampon onto the car seat that she sat on. She cried when she said that "Frank wouldn't help me. He left me sitting there in a pool of blood."

Sarah came through the screen door and saw the look on her parents' faces. "What's the matter," she asked as she kissed Pat on the cheek. Frank looked worried; his thoughts were elsewhere. He sat back down on the sofa. Sarah watched the news on the television and her parent's reactions. Pat told Frank that she watched several uniformed police officers outside the home of the woman who was killed.

"A vicious attack," were the reporter's words at the scene. Suddenly, Pat's brow sank. She had a thought and she wrote it down. She opened the drawer of the old wooden coffee table in front of the sofa. In it she found a pen, and she also found a school paper, which belonged to Boris. She twinged after she opened it. She saw that he got an "F," but much worse, was what she read:

"Don't ever laugh when a hearse goes by, or you may be the next to die. They wrap you up in a bloody sheet and send you down six-million feet. The worms go in and the words go out. They eat your intestines and spit them out. Your eyes pop out, your teeth decay and that's the end of a happy day."

Frank read the note as the screen door opened. Their eyes focused on Boris who, casually, entered. Sarah watched her parents who looked like they'd seen a ghost. They both turned pale as Boris smirked and asked: "What the hell's wrong with you?" Pat and Frank looked at each other for a second. Frank said that he asked him what he did that day. He replied, according Pat, that he "did nothing."

"Weren't you at school?" He looked at Pat, who said: "Oh, I told him this morning that he didn't have to go if he didn't want to."

Frank communicated: "Well, if you weren't in school then where were you?" Silence filled the room and everything was still.

"Why the questions," Boris asked? "What do you mean bombarding me with - where you been! I don't have to tell you where I've been." "I'd like to hear what other activities you had today, that's all," Frank recounted on the witness stand.

"Why?" Boris asked his father.

"No reason, son. Just checking on your well-being, that's all," Frank replied.

"When did you ever give a fuck about my well-being," he shot back.

"I should take off my leather belt," the angered father said as he gritted his teeth.

"Well go ahead, Frank, take it off," Boris taunted.

"Boris, did you know that the old lady was killed, Pat interjected?"

"What old lady," he quipped.

Pat looked at Frank for his reaction. Her eyes, immediately, shifted to Boris, and she said: "You know, the old lady we see out the kitchen window, sometimes."

"I don't know who you're talking about," he uttered, and went down the hall, into his room and closed the door. Sarah looked frightened as she watched. Her dad, she told Sam, comforted her, that everything would be okay. Both adults rose and walked into the kitchen. The agreement they came to took less than ten-seconds. Frank quietly retrieved a padlock from the kitchen utility drawer. Sarah walked into the room; she saw the padlock. She stopped her father and asked: "Can I stay overnight at Peggy's house?" Frank nodded and began to walk down the hallway to Boris' room. The closer he got the slower he crept until he was within a yard of Boris' bedroom door. Then he hesitated. He looked back and forth. The fearful father expressed his reality to be that all signs flashed red. He debated for a few seconds, moved closer, and then he carefully placed the padlock on the door, *where it should've been,* his M-team registered the thought.

Frank stated that the lock was removed the prior week because Boris argued that he would do better if it wasn't there. That day, however, before he brought the padlock together and locked it, suddenly, Boris tried to open the door."

"What the hell's going on? What are you doing?" Boris frantically pulled at the doorknob. "Why are you doing this? I haven't done anything wrong!" He, repeatedly, banged on the door with his fists.

"I locked him in his bedroom, and then I called the police," he told Sam. "Our suspicion sprang up when he denied even knowing of the old lady. We all knew her."

After the police arrived, Boris calmed down. The officers asked Frank if he ever had any guns in the house. He replied: "No guns." He paused and thought and remembered: "He owns a hunting knife." Two Police Officers had their guns drawn as they made their way down the hall. Frank slowly approached the door, and he knocked.

"Yes," the disturbed son calmly answered.

"Boris, the police are here. They want to talk to you," Frank said.

"Why do they want to talk to me?" he asked.

Frank looked at one of the officers; he shook his head.

"They're canvassing the neighborhood. They need to talk to everyone," Frank said.

"Is that why you locked me in?" he asked.

One of the officers had a loud, deep and commanding voice. "We want you spread out on the floor, face down, understand?"

There was a second of silence before he said: "Yes, sir."

Frank unlocked the padlock and removed it. The officer pushed the door open; its hinges creaked. Boris was face down; he spread out as if he just made an angel in the snow. "Where's the knife," one officer asked?

"What knife," he asked?

"The hunting knife," the Officer replied.

"I sold it," he said. Frank covertly looked at the other Office; he very lightly shook his head side to side.

The officer frisked him, cuffed him and then stood him up.

"Am I being arrested," Boris asked?

They each took one of the sixteen-year-old arms and led him out of the room.

The interrogation room was cold and compact. The ceiling was low. The fluorescent light omitted a low buzz as it shone over Boris; it made his shaggy hair shine. From the teenager's claustrophobic expression, the length and width of the room intimidated him. His juvenile eyes darted every-which-way as he looked for the camera. He sat in a hard chair which was bolted to the floor. He sat erect. His hands folded together in front of him as if he was a very good boy.

Detective John Wicks was a seasoned interrogator with a very professional manner. He introduced himself, cordially, to the young man seated in front of him. His words formed sentences as if he was a graceful ballerina; he danced divinely. He was a master of his art. He strung words together and delivered them in a manner that commanded transfixed attention.

I watched the interrogation on YouTube, because I never understood my nephew's motive. I needed to get inside of his mind. I never understood his pathetic path. Why was he on it? What put him there? Boris knew right from wrong. He took away a life. It was an unspeakable crime. Another said: "When a person hits the age of ninety, they must be a pretty good person. Centenarians, even more so." Why did Boris desire the death of a ninety-year-old woman? What wedged in his mind and kept the crack open in himself? Why did it widen?

Boris decided to play the "I don't know what you're talking about card. Detective Wicks had seen it all. He decided to roll-up his sleeves. There was a long night ahead. He called his wife before it started because already, he knew. "You don't need to stay up. I'll be late." He ended the call. He read the investigators report. There were no witnesses. The crime took place at the time of day most people worked. Malefic's report outlined the crime scene investigation. It was classified as first-degree murder. "It was a crime of rage," the news reports announced. An expert, who was interviewed said: "It had a vindictive and evil twist to it." The killer read, looked and listened to morbidity. It pushed him out of his fantasy world. He acted it all out, in his mind, exactly what he wanted to do. He already responded to internal stimuli a great deal about it. He was now motivated and prepared. He commanded it. He yearned for it in his heart. He swished fantasy's around in his mind for months. He felt good when he did it. He possessed the evil power of a sadist. But Wicks decided to play the boy's hubris.

He asked the young man: "Tell me what you know about assassins." The word brought out a kind of sensuality in Boris' eyes. Wicks knew that the youth lived in a world where only monsters felt comfortable. Wicks felt it wise, so he bypassed the "you'll feel much better if you confess," approach. He also sidetracked on the "do you want people to think you're a monster?" Lastly, the interrogator decided to nix the "there's two sides to every story. I want to hear yours." Wicks used those tactics before, and in that scenario, he said things like: "Maybe it was an accident. Maybe it was in self-defense." No, the detective had been around long enough. He grasped the depths that the human mind sunk to, sometimes. He understood evil. He saw its power as he worked. He noticed how the mind sickened when fed a steady diet of misinformation, horror, and criminality. Wicks knew about the hands, which reached into a young person's mind. It was to be massaged. It was mentored. It was to be peppered with the spices of evil.

Boris was told that his mother feared him, and he smirked. He expressed intense interest when told he had the pulse of an assassin according to his medical information. Boris bought into it. He said: "The way you look at the world is the way you see it." Wicks granted the youngster's permission, and he hopped aboard a lane only the assassin took. He confirmed the high level of importance that he had placed on himself. The kid loosened up. He became more animated. He explained that he looked at humanity through a special lens. One only he accessed and controlled. He was a master, but he never acknowledged that he was the killer of a 90-year-old woman, at home, with her television on.

Wicks knew what he was up against. He felt it necessary to feed the boy's ego. For hours he answered questions. Wicks was tireless to the end. He worked on the boy just like a great artist worked on a painting, a little bit at a time. He gained the confession of the young man. He was some kind of superstar. Once into the suspect's mindset he asked Boris why he was so proficient at what he did. He replied that he never understood what he learned and why he learned. He answered that he read about military training. Along with his interest in the martial arts. It got him to talk about what he was interested in. Television, movies, videos and video games? The youngster professed his knowledge.

"It was just mental focus. I've studied things that I should've not studied." He boasted that no one taught him anything. Wicks wondered, out loud: "Where did you learn to stab like that?" "You know, like, some people get it and some don't."

"I didn't," he admitted. Wicks wanted him to explain the technique he used when he stabbed. He replied: "It was nothing fancy." He told Wicks that somewhere in the subconscious of his mind he developed the skills of an assassin, but "with no training. The knowledge just came to him," he boasted.

I concluded that his mind and heart were sickened by the sort of proclivities he was exposed to in his environment. *Malefic* quantified his data. The young man flirted with darkness. He consciously chose evil. And it was all due to the fact his *M-planner, M-developer* and *M-coordinator* had pegged him for an institutional life behind bars.

Pat's alcoholism and her Pliartrum drug addiction took a turn for the worse; she was arrested on a DUI. When she worked, she drank and smoked. So, when she got into her car and drove home every night; it was bound to happen. Frank bailed her out. When I went to Boris' sentencing hearing, she looked ill. Frank looked embarrassed to be there.

Boris appeared in an orange jumpsuit and chains as he entered the courtroom. The teen looked less defiant. He was born Boris Karloff Isaac. Frank told me it was "so cool to pick out a newborn's name." He felt that he honored Boris by giving him the name. "It did," according to Pat. They watched old horror movies from the 1930s and 40s together when he was young. "Frankenstein, The Bride of Frankenstein, and the Son of Frankenstein were honored movies in the household. Boris was a difficult child to raise." He was born unwanted which impacted the family nucleus. He was ignored more than he was loved. He was disciplined and punished almost daily. He was rarely rewarded with something. Frank and Pat raised him like they were raised. They expected him to succeed, but he skirted their expectations. He dropped out of high school in the tenth grade. "But he earned his GED," she defended. The boy stood taller than Frank, who was six-feet-three inches. He was good looking, and the girls liked him. So, something went wrong in Doctor Frankenstein's laboratory, I thought.

When I "traveled" I always made a stop at Frank's. They put me in the extra bedroom once. I stayed in the notorious basement every other time. In the cellar, my cluster headaches and depression were very bad. One night, I had another cluster headache. I had nothing to fight it with. In addition, my lower back went out, and I had to pee. It was all at the same time. Pinned to the floor I dragged myself to the bathroom. Without doubt, it could have won the prize as the worst experience in my whole, excuse the profanity, fucking life. One day, in the morning, when I was in the guest room, I heard through my closed bedroom door the struggle between an addicted mother and her dysfunctional son. Pat said things like: "If you don't go to school then you can't have any dessert tonight. I made an apple pie." He retorted: "I don't care. I don't want to go to school." Frank and Pat were pushed to the limit and attended a few emergency parent/teacher conferences over the years. The father always told the boy: "I never, in my life, had a parent/teacher conference; emergency or not."

When they lived out in Patriot Park, Pat told me that Boris liked to trap small rodents with a cardboard box. One year, Frank bought him a small trap for his birthday. The main problems that Boris had centered around Frank, and his inept parenting. Frank's indifference, Pat's alcoholism, along with her use of Pliartrum's drugs, created the perfect storm. They were too loose with Boris. He was allowed to run roughshod in the home. Frank told him: "when you were a youngster a disturbed stork brought you to us." The misshapen mind believed it. When he got older the "philosopher," said one day: "I don't like being human. I'd rather have been a part of the bird or lizard world; he said that it would be "real cool to be a vulture or a Komodo Dragon."

Boris faced the music that day. It lasted more than an hour. It took place in the same courtroom where he was tried and found guilty. The kid faced the death penalty or life in prison without parole. I talked to him about it. Because his mother and father never did, since the guilty verdict. They never loved him, and they showed it. Sarah was off at college. She was in her freshman year, studying to be a nurse, something she always wanted to be.

My presence, at the sentencing hearings, helped nothing. The young man's eyes looked defiant. The Honorable Judge who rose above him entered, which followed the Bailiff's announcement. We all stood until the judge took his seat and gaveled in. The court sentencing allowed different family and friends, who were believably broken-hearted, over the manner of their loved one's deaths. For people who died because of natural causes, or even after a long illness; it was easier to cope with. When murdered, everyone who knew the victim felt horrible for her, and themselves as if it had happened to them.

Boris sat, erect, at his Defense Council's table. His head darted like a dog. He was flanked by his attorney, a public defender. The prosecutor sat adjacent to the defense. He represented the State. I sat in the courtroom crowded by the press, family and friends of the deceased.

I thought about it. It sent my mind back to the time I watched the full interrogation of Boris. Detective Wicks was fantastic. He circled the boy as if he was a giant anaconda, and it wrapped around its prey before he went in for the kill. He stroked the boy's ego from the second he walked into that interrogation room. He soon got him to talk. The detective told Boris:

"Wow! You're confident, cool, and unique. Where did you obtain the knowledge to do all of this? Were you watching stuff?"

"No," Boris replied, "the knowledge just comes to me." He went on: "I've developed myself as an assassin."

"Did you have training," he asked the boy?

"No, it was from my imagination," he replied.

"Where did you get the knife," Wicks inquired?

"From my Aunt Glenda," he responded.

Both cops looked at Frank at the same time. The father of the boy shook his head and rolled his eyes.

Chapter 3

Samuel Isaac started at the bottom of a new career field. Literally, he moved into a cheap basement apartment of an old Victorian home. He noticed across the street there was a stretch of old-fashioned rowhomes, the kind that had a great porche. One stood out. Quite a few people came and went through its door. It happened throughout the day. Sam took a breath of fresh air as he emerged from the cellar. He picked up a newspaper at the corner store. He went to the help wanted ads. He was in poor shape, both physically and mentally, and his only job experience was as an administrative clerk in the navy. When he found an ad for a clerk typist he knew right away that he qualified for the job because he had that four-year degree. However, at this point and time, he thought the degree meant nothing. In fact, if he revealed it when interviewed he thought the employer probably wouldn't have hired him because with his degree he could be employed anywhere doing anything.

The Meyer's Club was a long-standing social service agency. It was started in the 1960s, it provided therapeutic programs for social, recreational and life skills to adults with mental illness. Sam remembered when he first crossed the threshold of its door. He had no idea that he had just entered the Twilight Zone, better known as the MH (mental health) world. The help-wanted ad listed an address to apply at. It was that old row home which was directly across the street; it was that home that Sam identified early on with all of the comings and goings everyday. He stood outside and looked across the street at it. A sizable *Stars and Stripes* flag was displayed outside the home. On the great porch there was a big blue placard sign on the wall next to the entryway. It read: *Meyer's Club - where friendship begins, and loneliness ends.*

His commute to work became a running joke with him because the next day, when he emerged from the underground apartment, he was wearing a shirt and tie and carrying a folder. He walked from one side of the street to the other complaining to himself that getting to work was such a pain in the ass. The interview went well. The Program Director hired Sam for the job of clerk typist in the program's administrative office.

The Meyer's Club was a special place. It was a mental health program for (SMI) severely mentally ill adults who lived in the community. The drop-in center was patronized by many. They all came for different reasons. While some folks sat and watched television, others engaged in the programs that were planned, developed, and coordinated to enhance a mentally ill person's quality of life. There were many social, recreational, and life skills programs everyday. Many took advantage of the free lunch. The lunch room was filled everyday.

Sam was to have a career in the MH world, and pathways were quickly developed for him by his M-team. From the M-planners, M-developers, and M-coordinators to his M-watchers and M-workers it was all planned and choreographed by the great supernatural system.

He never realized it but when he walked upon the pathway it was for his benefit of himself and others. The pathway led him to the door of an honorable career. Early on, however, as he walked on, he began to recognize his behaviors in others which only managed to confuse him more. He learned that the narratives of the people he served were no different than his. These folks were hurt and traumatized.

To Sam, it was all very disturbing and tragic. Time passed and through it the MH worker watched Malefic's magic as it worked on souls weakened by mental illness; his own being one of them. Sam Isaac learned many lessons both on and off the job. The lessons helped him develop his inner strength. He took advantage of the education and he passed it on to others. The learning experience provided him with a great opportunity. It was to be the avenue that moved him forward towards reconciliation and healing. He was to help himself and the people he served, so they all gained, understood, and developed an awareness about their MH diagnosis and condition. It was the individual's treatment plan that helped and empowered Sam and his MH clients at the Meyer's Club, and as a result, they grew inside which demonstrated because they heeded their impulses which was to help them through their thoughts, as they slowly healed and their quality of life improved.

The career was meant for Sam; it fit him like a glove. He had a new vocation, one which he was unprepared and uneducated for. Gradually, his new life unfolded in front of him. However, deep down, Sam never knew it, but he was very natural at guiding others. His new career addressed his depressed inner self which he held on for so very long.

It was a non-stop journey of enlightenment and tragedy, an education on goodness. But the road twisted and turned as Sam tried to get there. There were potholes and detour signs. All traffic lights turned red, and obstacles were placed on the path. And, later, at times, his career traveled across an endless road filled with misery, pain, and mileage. To start the fantastic journey Sam needed, as said before, a bachelor's degree; it helped him get a job in the business world, but he knew nothing about what to do with it otherwise. Malefic connected to the M-team. M-workers were ordered to begin.

The help-wanted ad listed an address to apply at. It was directly across the street; it was that home that Sam identified where all of the comings and goings. Sam stood outside and looked across the street at it. A sizable *Stars and Stripes* was attached outside the home. There was a big blue placard sign on the wall next to the entryway. It read: *Meyer's Club - where friendship begins, and loneliness ends.* Sam was hired for the clerk typist position in the administrative office of a MH program for chronically mentally ill adults who lived in the community. The Meyer's Club was a long-standing social service agency. It was started in the 1960s, it provided therapeutic programs for social, recreational and life skills to adults with mental illness. Sam remembered when he first crossed the threshold of its door. He had no idea that he had just entered the Twilight Zone, better known as the MH (mental health) world.

Sam's life was upended numerous times. An edict was issued through Malefic, which meant higher authority had been consulted. With his first step he forged a path into the volatile world of the human mind and human behavior. It was both wonderful and nightmarish; the secrets held by the soul. From the deepest part of hell to the highest cloud in heaven, Sam cleared the branches that clouded his vision into life. What he discovered; however, outdid everything that he lost. He faced an arduous and laborious journey up steep mountains, and across great deserts and vast oceans. If he was incarcerated, he accomplished nothing; nothing good that is. He was humbled, nevertheless, by the change because he never wanted to go to his grave with nothing but regrets. The opportunity presented itself and Sam welcomed it; he was to be a contributor to the good from that moment on while he lived.

Sam was quickly hired for the clerk typist position in the administrative office of a MH program for chronically mentally ill adults who lived in the community. The Meyer's Club was a long-standing social service agency. It was started in the 1960s, it provided therapeutic programs for social, recreational and life skills to adults with mental illness. Sam remembered when he first crossed the threshold of its door. He had no idea that he had entered the MH world. He would never have fathomed that it was to be his future.

Sam had arrived where he established his career, and even more importantly, it established a path. He attempted to do better; somehow, he was made aware, and his inner-self and physical-self connected, and as a result, he was given access to Malefic's helpful information.

The new MH worker taught the information to many MH members during his first MH job when he was a Therapeutic Rehabilitation Specialist with the Meyer's Club. As Sam understood it and later explained that our inner self, the soul, and our physical self were brought together when we're born. Consequently, the two entities were united. But if there ever was conflict between self and soul, then that created a split; a division, which paved the way for Sam to use the concept that echoed a World War I slogan: *United We Stand. Divided We Fall.*

It wasn't too long after he started at his new job that he recognized that he had mental illness. He understood that he was depressed. Sam sought help outside the club. Time passed and he thought that he got better, because he responded to the antidepressant medication. But much later he learned, the hard way, that he only put a *Band-Aid* on a nasty wound.

Sam remained the clerk typist for about two months. One day he borrowed the ear of a very nice man. He was the Executive Director of the Meyer's Club. "I'd like to work with the members," Sam told him. The Director agreed and permitted it. The ex-clerk typist gave up the position to become a therapeutic-recreation prograM-developer. Translation: He started his MH career from the very bottom.

Sam listened to folks who were, usually, ignored. The way he thought that he saw himself, years later, was that he listened to the ignored because they had interesting things to talk about. He heard them and responded to them with empathy, advice, and goodwill. Sam had a way about him. He never realized it, but he had a calm bedside manner; it was like he was a medical doctor while he worked. When there was any kind of conflict, within people's self or with others, he lowered the temperature. For the first time in his life; he felt respected. When he worked with his peers he learned along with them. He was the inept one. He was the one who never had a real friend. He had a lot of problems but looking back, he recognized

Sam felt comfortable there. He recognized it as his career early on. He admitted, to himself, that he understood that he had problems, and that he was on the right path to find the answers that he sought about himself and life. Early on he realized that he had a few extra layers of compassion. Maybe it was because he was one of them. He never talked about it but something hit him on his first day of the job.

From the beginning, Malefic's choreography was not obvious to Sam when he processed that day later in life. He was cleared for assignment. He was chosen. He worked with those who were diagnosed with a serious mental illness. He listened, watched and learned. In his new job he planned and carried out social, recreational and life skills programs. For the first few months he worked with goodhearted people who were developmentally delayed. Their programming included programs like bowling or swimming at the Jewish Community Center. Feeding the ducks at Italian lake. Walking along the riverfront. Going to movies and restaurants. Using Bingo, Uno, and other board games of chance and competition which acted in the capacity as their social, recreational, and life skills programming.

The months passed and there was turnover in the ranks. The adult MH therapeutic recreational coordinator gave notice and left the club. Sam applied for the position, and he was hired. He understood and took the job seriously. In his mind, it was an important job. He accepted and embraced the world that he now lived and worked in. However, it was at this point there was a problem. It was the life skills part. Sam knew nothing. He knew if he shoplifted that he would be caught, and if he stole anything else; it wasn't any different.

There were no other lessons that he had learned. He had nothing to offer, so Sam learned as they learned. In groups he presented skills from a teacher's manual. There was always a discussion on each topic they learned. When with the members, he socialized freely, for the first time in his life, but as the boss; it helped a lot, long before he learned the naked truth. For the first time in his life he felt comfortable around others and tolerated himself. Still, it was only when he worked. When he went home, he stayed to himself.

Over a span of thirty-years, however, when he worked in MH field, both on and off job; he was in constant MH mode. He never knew it. He never practiced it. It just happened automatically. Day after day, week after week, month after month, and year after year Sam's verbal and nonverbal communication skills were his keys to his success.

The good world was very contagious but not as contagious as the bad world. Everyday, Sam brought the veneer of goodness into every moment he served others. It was that look in his eyes, and the sound of his voice in knowing, understanding, and communicating to others that he knew what he was talking about, and that children and adults responded in kind; they showed their goodness which each individual had an abundance of.

Children and adults responded to Sam's message of taking constant stock of themselves and showing an equal amount of tolerance in their energy toward others. Goodness was in Sam's eyes and he got it right back and then some everyday. The contagion spread through groups like a wildfire. Malefic's report indicated that Sam was at his best everyday in his career because he genuinely cared about the people he served; he wanted them to understand themselves to bring it succeed and to learn about the great dichotomy inside them, and how, not only, to bring it together and to sell it pass it on to others with great eaze. And as a teacher, Sam refused to accept anything different because, for whatever reason. Because he was chosen to teach the young and old about their life in general. There were many people who needed his services and he delivered those services, without much of an effort, every time.

It all started at the Meyer's Club with the MH adults that he held sway over.

He never knew that he had only two-years at the club, before he moved on to a different MH assignment. Sam's path included a new tool that M-workers installed in him. The cluster headache entered his life. M-workers were ordered, at first, that he be awakened each night with tremendous pressure and powerful pain in his brain. It stabbed him repeatedly in the same eye, forty, fifty, sometimes sixty minutes or more. Sam reported that the pain felt like it was inflicted by an icepick. The source of what caused cluster headaches remained unknown to the medical world. It took Sam decades until he understood; it was Malefic. Sam's lifelong overseer had only opened doors of criminality and deceitfulness to him but now it was time for him to see his other half.

Nothing good was open to him. When he tried toward the good, he was always stopped; it never worked out. Not when he was a kid. Sam recalled when he wanted to attend Hebrew School or *Yeshiva*. What he wanted was shot down. In fact, he remembered that Dorothy laughed when Poppa said: "So, you want to be a Yeshiva boy." Poppa acted like he was dovening in prayer, as he laughed. In fact, everybody in the room laughed except Sam.

His religious needs were ignored. The fellowship that he tore up came from the heart. He wanted to live in Israel, following his graduation from college. He never realized his goal. He failed when he was arrested for shoplifting which Malefic, finally, ordered to put a halt to Sam's thievery, and it did, and it was a long time coming courtesy of Malefic.

Malefic blocked Sam a third time, as well. His path toward religion was halted. As a kid he reached out to it, but he experienced a great void. His heart emptied, but it continued to beat even though it was bone dry. He remembered that he stepped back two-steps, but he never found the new path, and he never proceeded. He was frozen, religiously.

It was upon his departure from the Meyer's Club that he moved right into another position. When he gave notice at a job and departed, there was a period that he never worked. It was down-time. But, as soon as he could, usually, two-years later, he bounced back, and when he did, he found a completely different job, although the positions, all except for two, were always in the MH field. Sam did fine for two-years or so, then he petered out. He quit. He uprooted himself and he "traveled." He never understood why? He knew zilch, which forced M-workers into major surgery.

Sam's lessons and punishment lasted for decades. Cluster headaches "traveled" along with him everywhere he went. Usually, for some people, it was nice to have a companion on a trip. Sam, at those times, would have been better off dead. But he kept going. He "traveled" only with Rusty and his possessions. Sam's dog was always by his side. When the ledgers were tallied at autopsy. There were four breaks, over thirty-years. Each break lasted a couple of years; it took Sam to depths that he could never have imagined.

But Sam always rebounded. Soon after he found employment again. It was another MH job. He worked in another capacity in the MH world. His MH transitions began at the Meyer's Club. Two-years after he arrived he, suddenly, one day he followed a whim. He gave notice. He moved to another state. He left the club for no reason. He liked being there. People liked him and he liked them. But he moved on. He had a big sendoff at the club and the members gave him a beautiful gift, a very nice briefcase made of soft leather. In those two years at the club he did things that he never did before. Things that were social and recreational. Experiences he never had because Tony ruined Sam's ability to make friends and have close relations with his peers..

For example, once a month, without a date; he never had one; Sam took a group of Meyer Club members to a nightclub where there was a live band. The members, Sam included, danced until the wee hours of the morning. Nobody drank alcohol, just sodas; however, it was their choice. The program was very well received. Sam also had, to his credit, many educational and recreational programs he planned, coordinated, and carried out. The groups traveled to Washington, D.C. to the Smithsonian Museums and the National Zoo. They traveled up to Mystic Seaport in Connecticut, where they toured an old whaling ship, and ate clam chowder at a chowder festival. It was all business but it was all Malefic.

But the lesson that he learned and relayed to himself was encrypted for the longest time; he had no access prior to it. Sam packed up and moved to a town in another state. He was hired, rather quickly, for his second MH job after the club. He was a MH technician. He served SMI (seriously mentally ill) adults at the State psychiatric hospital in Las Vegas, Nevada. The patients were there, because they had a MH crisis. Sam followed orders from the psychiatric nurses. He spent most of his time out amongst the patients. He conducted a bed-check every fifteen-minutes. Some patients were asleep in their rooms. Others watched television, and some walked, slowly, back and forth through the hallways. The job was short because three months later, he was hired as a Teaching Parent Relief for the State residential treatment program for kids. In the second job, he worked with (SED) severely emotionally disturbed children aged seven to sixteen.

But he packed his bags 4 years later. He moved on; he felt compelled to do so.. Again, it was part of the cycle. He never understood or questioned the transitions. Sam determined, years later, that Malefic gave him a taste of his own medicine when it came to working with the SED kids. The temptation to show him how, as a child, he was mistreated; his parents neglected him. His behavior was very poor prior to age 8. He was out of control. This all paved the way for Sam to see a psychologist at the State Hospital, who told Dorothy that Sam was a perfectly normal kid.

Dorothy and Eric had a hard time believing what the doctor said.

But the mental health education and the human inner-growth was too tempting a morsel for Malefic to pass up. Malefic knew that he had a young Jewish male with the diagnosis, prior to age 8, as having conduct disorder and that a bipolar diagnosis would be added as well. Aviodant personality disorder, which he developed after his bar-mitzvah was the fourth. Next, at age 18, he would receive his ASPD, cluster B, sociopath which was preceded by his conduct disorder. Sam took 9 medications. Four of them were for his psychiatric disorders.

He, thankfully, finished his second stop on the tour. Having brought Sam into this line of work the M-team called the shots. Eventually, Sam learned that he was on the MH tour, and it lasted for three decades.

Sam held six positions in three states. He was employed in a seventh and eighth job, but they weren't all in the MH field. He learned, but then he suffered. He "traveled" for punishment, not pleasure. For many months, over many decades, the cluster headache pain continued. Conveniently, when he was between jobs; it, got even worse. He "traveled" only in the spring and summer. These whims never came in the dead of winter. His downtime, in his warped mind, totaled forty-thousand miles, which was driven in three separate cars over the time span. Two of them looked like broken down junk cars. But they never broke down. They leaked a ton of oil. He carried a few quarts and a gallon of water with him all the time. One vehicle's engine overheated. He'd have to pull over to put water into it. But, once he was in a traffic jam, on a freeway, as he drove out of San Francisco. The needle stayed at high. The traffic barely moved for minutes on end. Sam was frantic. He was sure it would break down. He had no air conditioning. The windows were down, and it was in the middle of summer, and the needle didn't budge. It never went higher; but it never decreased. Sam and Rusty worried. The dog owner surmised during this time there would be this nightmarish scene with him and Rusty, stuck in the middle of a sea of motor vehicles. Thanks to the M-workers, who worked regularly on automotive vehicles and their mechanical issues but the car never overheated to the point it broke down.

He had his road trips down to a science because he did it so often. Sam was always packed with all his personal possessions, kitchen odds-and-ends, four large boxes filled with VHS tapes, a VCR, television set, a ton of clothes, and most importantly, Rusty. The man and his dog went through state after state around and around the country. He only stopped at night. He always had a room in a franchised establishment. Sam and Rusty ate fast food all the time. He drove about five-hundred-miles per day. He never stayed long wherever he went. Pennsylvania to Nevada, to California back to Pennsylvania, then down to Florida, and back to Nevada once again. Sam repeated this process four times, although he only went to the deep south of the continent once.

He received a Social Security disability check every month. Prior to 2016, he was diagnosed with depression. After that the diagnosis was changed to bipolar. Before he "traveled" he saw a psychologist. Sam was back on psychotropic medications which the patient had stopped. He moved to Florida for seven-months. He lived with, and tolerated, these zig-zag moves back and forth for endless hours and miles. He always "traveled" on the Interstate Highway System. He was all over the nation, and he was tired. He pledged to himself no more moves. He settled in for a few years in different MH jobs. He broke his pledge; consequently, he was back on the road again shortly after.. Years later, Sam was accompanied by his nemesis, the cluster headache. It kicked his ass day and night. Sam hated life. However, his greatest contempt was saved for the cluster headaches attacks he had while he drove. Those were all really bad. He cradled his head as he drove on. The pain was unbelievable, and he wasn't doing himself any favors. At that time, he smoked cigarettes, which only heightened the pain.

After he resigned from my State position with SED kids, he was in poor physical shape. Cluster headaches happened day and night. He was still on Social Security Disability, but he was allowed to supplement the benefit. He worked a part-time job. Without doubt, I\he understood years later, it was Malefic and his M-team who tortured Sam and facilitated everything. The M-team laid out the blueprint for his next four years.

For the first two years, he learned lessons hinged to HIS homosexuality. The studio apartment that he obtained in Las Vegas, was a block away from the gay-bar district. The most popular drinking establishment sat next to a small video store. Video Rentals had regular movie VHS tapes to rent, but in the back, there was a sizable array of heterosexual and homosexual pornographic VHS tapes to rent or buy. They had a help-wanted sign in the store's window. Sam was hired on the spot, and he began his part-time job the next day.

M-planners, M-developers and M-coordinators had shifted into another area because he still hadn't learned my lesson about his homosexuality.

The months he worked there were of educational value. M-workers collected a great deal of data, which showed that he was totally dysfunctional sociality. He had a lot of sex, but there was no love. He cried over the phone to Frank about his problems, and how he felt as he worked there. Sam soon "traveled" again. This time it was short; only one-thousand miles. He returned to Las Vegas and the video store. Three months later he left their employment again and "traveled."

The next time he rebounded, it took a while. His new studio apartment was in another area of town. Sam was well, mentally, and he became an elementary school substitute teacher. Two years later, he obtained another State MH position and left another noble profession, teaching, back to his other area: mental health.

The reason he became a substitute teacher was because there was a State hiring freeze. In his first year, as a teacher, he struggled. He was overweight, and he had just recovered from the last grueling road trip; it crisscrossed the nation three-times. Granted, it was the longest one of them all. But he was hired as a substitute based solely on the fact that he had a bachelor's degree. It didn't matter what it was in. Malefic's theory panned out; Sam did need that piece of paper after all. He had never stood in front of a classroom filled with children as an adult. He worked with mentally ill kids at his last MH job. But it was different this time. He realized, years later, that he was like a star; all eyes were drawn to me because of his position as the teacher. Kids, Sam discovered, looked to adults for knowledge. They wanted more than the ABCs. At his last MH position, he implemented the mentally ill children's individual treatment plans. Sure, the staff tried to teach other things: self-esteem, etc. In school, however, Sam learned that they looked for more than just a regular education.

It was during his first weeks, of being a substitute, that things went haywire. One day, the substitute teacher must have displayed non-verbal communication i.e. an expression that he was mad at something. It and along with my words, did the trick. He taught nothing good that day to the class of fourth graders because those actions led to something bad. The kids placed a note on the teacher's desk when he wasn't looking that said: "We hate you." At the end of the day, the downtrodden sub wrote a note to the teacher about it. He felt hurt. The incident shook me. He must have processed it in his mind rather quickly because soon after he joined a gym, things started to change. One morning, when he showered something happened. A touch of wisdom came to him. He worked on it relentlessly. As the excess weight melted off, he carried on, he built upon the words, and he ran them over and over in his mind. It became monumental.

Sam was assisted and he experienced a remarkable transformation. The weirdest thing was, years later, after he worked for the State with SED kids, he came home from another day at school. There was a young man seated on the concrete steps of Sam's apartment building; he sat next to a ten-gallon aquarium. There was a sizable turtle in it. The young man asked: "Want a turtle?" I remembered next that he heard: "You're, Sam Isaac." The kid added, "You're looking good."

Sam looked at him with raised eyebrows and asked: "How do you know my name?" It turned out that he was one of the kids that Sam served when he worked at State with SED MH diagnosis. It was ten-years ago, when the boy was thirteen. Immediately after the kid told me his name, Sam instantly remembered him. The teacher and his pupil shared a little conversation over the smoking of some marijuana in Sam's apartment. Of course, if he was thirteen-years-of-age, Sam should've never smoked or especially, given it to him the way Glenda gave to Sam, all those years ago. It was remarkable to see him. Firstly, he looked nothing like he did as a young teenager. It was funny because the image in Sam's mind, at that time, pictured the young man as a boy. So, as he sat in front of Sam it was a strange feeling to understand our history. He talked about his life. Sam knew the circumstances of how and why he entered the State's residential, behavioral program. Gene battled with life just like everybody did.

These were good times. Sam was in good physical and mental shape; Marijuana was back in his life because the cluster headaches never left him. The plant was made by *Mother Nature*. It helped Sam cope with agony. He stopped smoking cigarettes, months ago, and replaced it with cannabis. The plant, as indicated before, helped him. Not everybody who had cluster headaches found that cannabis helped the condition. In one study, only twenty-five percent found it helped. On the other end of the spectrum there were twenty-five percent who reported that it made the headaches worse for them. While the majority of cluster headache people, fifty percent, said that it made no difference at all. It didn't help them. But it didn't hurt. The pain went on. Sam used what worked, the cannabis, because he finally found a steady supplier. He was the first person that Sam bought it from on a consistent basis. Every time he needed it he was there. It allowed him to fight the torture. And Sam started to turn the tables, and eventually, he gained the upper hand over them. He still got them, but he fought them; it was war, and he was winning for once.

Malefic, however, had new plans for Sam. The State had lifted its hiring-freeze. The substitute teacher was soon hired by another division within the State MH System. Sam became a psychiatric caseworker. He was given a caseload of chronically mentally ill adults who he worked with. Sam helped them with all their business. Landlord problems, social security matters, trouble at the bank, etc. But he also presented, to the clients, the States MH psychosocial rehabilitation program. He taught adults in groups. It was life skills training, and he added his little shtick, from the classroom, as he taught their lessons. Sam learned from the program that he taught. They were basic common-sense topics: Socialization, communication, coping skills, etc. Eventually, Sam finished at that clinic. The collected data indicated that Malefic had transitioned Sam again. This time it was an assignment at another clinic. He performed the same duties but, only weeks after he arrived; he ruined it or Malefic ruined it.

He had an explosive episode; it never happened to him before. Sam blew up. There were no clients at this brand-new clinic he was assigned to. The roster wasn't fully staffed yet. One day, as he sat at the front desk; he was bored. He remembered that he twiddled with a paperclip. During it the M-workers acted. It was something that he did and said to a coworker. She told Sam that she hated the classical music that he put on in the waiting room. The psychiatric caseworker II bolted out of his chair, and he told the coworker that she hated everything, and he stormed back to his office. The next day, Sam was told that he was being disciplined. Then, for the first time in my MH career, he really lost it. He yelled out: "I quit."

Disturbed, he frantically went into his office and took down every drawing that the kids in the elementary schools had drawn for him. He was caked into his sickness. He threw the gifts out when he got home. They were a tool that he used. He had them tacked up all over the wall space, so when he met with clients for individual one on one psycho-social rehabilitation sessions he found they worked because they meant so much to Sam.

Sam had his road trips down to a science because he did it so often. He was always packed with all his personal possessions, kitchen odds-and-ends, four large boxes filled with VHS tapes, a VCR, television set, a ton of clothes, and most importantly, Rusty. They went through state after state. San only stopped at night. He always had a room in a franchised establishment. He and Rusty ate fast food all the time. They drove about five-hundred-miles per day. He never stayed long. Pennsylvania to Nevada, to California back to Pennsylvania. Leaving the Golden State Sam moved for minutes on end. He was frantic. He was sure it would break down. He had no air conditioning. The windows were down, and it was in the middle of summer, and the needle didn't budge. It never went higher; but it never decreased. Me and Rusty worried. Sam surmised during this time there would be this nightmarish scene with him and Rusty, stuck in the middle of a sea of motor vehicles. Thanks to M-workers, who worked regularly on automotive vehicle issues and the car never overheated to the point it broke down. The high/low game repeated itself four times, and although he only went to the deep south of the continent once, it should have happened more.

Sam received a Social Security disability check every month. He was diagnosed with depression but it was changed to bipolar depression by the psychiatrist in 2016. Before Sam "traveled" he saw a psychologist. He was back on psychotropic medications, which he had stopped. He moved to Florida for seven-months. He lived with, and tolerated, these zig-zag moves back and forth for endless hours and miles. He always "traveled" on the Interstate Highway System. He was all over the nation, and he was exhausted. He pledged to himself; that he would never move again. He settled in for a few years in different MH jobs. Sam broke his pledge, and he was back on the road again doing the same things soon after. Years later, he was accompanied by his nemesis, the cluster headache. It kicked his ass day and night. Sam hated life. However, his greatest contempt was saved for the cluster attacks he had while he was driving. Those were all really bad. Sm cradled his head as he drove on. The pain was unbelievable, and he wasn't doing himself any favors. At that time, he smoked cigarettes, which only heightened the pain.

After he resigned from his State position with SED kids. He was in poor physical shape. Cluster headaches happened day and night. He was still on Social Security Disability, but he was allowed to supplement the benefit. He worked a part-time job. Without doubt, he understood, years later, it was Malefic and his team who tortured him and facilitated everything. Malefic laid out the blueprint for the next four years.

For the first two years, Sam learned lessons hinged to HIS homosexuality. The studio apartment that he moved into was a block away from the gay-bar district. The most popular drinking establishment sat next to a small video store. Video Rentals had regular movie VHS tapes to rent, but in the back, there was a sizable array of heterosexual and homosexual pornographic VHS tapes to rent or buy. They had a help-wanted sign in the store's window. Sam was hired on the spot, and he began his part-time job the next day.

M-planners, M-developers and M-coordinators had shifted into another area because he still hadn't learned my lesson about HIS homosexuality.

The months HE worked there were of educational value. M-workers collected a great deal of data, which showed that Sam was totally, socially, dysfunctional. He had a lot of sex, but there was no love. Sam cried over the phone to his younger brother about his problems, and how he felt as he worked at the video store. He "traveled" again. This time it was short; only one-thousand miles. He returned to Las Vegas and the video store. Three months later he left their employment, and "traveled" once again.

The next time he rebounded, it took a while. His new studio apartment was in another area of town. He was well, mentally, and he became an elementary school substitute teacher. Two years later, he obtained another State MH position and left another noble profession, teaching, back to another - mental health.

The reason Sam became a substitute teacher was because there was a State hiring freeze. In his first year, as a teacher; he struggled. He was overweight, and he had just recovered from the last grueling road trip; it crisscrossed the nation three-times. Granted, it was the longest one of them all. But Sam was hired as a substitute based solely on the fact that he had a bachelor's degree. It didn't matter what it was in. He had never stood in front of a classroom filled with children as an adult. Sam worked with mentally ill kids at his last MH job. But it was different this time. He realized, years later, that he was like a shiny star; all eyes were drawn to him because of his position as the teacher. He discovered that kids looked to adults for knowledge. They wanted more than the ABCs. At his last MH position, he implemented the mentally ill children's individual treatment plans. Sure, they tried to teach other things: self-esteem, socialization etc. In school, however, he learned that the kids looked for more than a regular education.

It was during Sam's first weeks, of being a substitute, that things went haywire. One day, Sam must have displayed non-verbal communication i.e. an expression that he was mad or something. The words he used must have confused whoever heard it. Sam taught nothing good that day to the class of fourth graders because those actions led to something bad. The kids placed a note on the desk when he wasn't looking that said: "We hate you." At the end of the day, Sam wrote a note to the teacher about it. He felt hurt. It shook me. He must have processed it in his mind rather quickly because soon after he joined a gym and things started to change. One morning, when he showered something happened. A touch of wisdom came to him. He worked on the wording relentlessly. As the excess weight melted off, he carried on and built upon the words, and he ran them over and over in his mind. It became a monumental moment.

Sam was assisted as he experienced the remarkable transformation. The weirdest thing was, years later, after he worked for the State with SED kids. He came home from another day at school. There was a young man seated on the concrete steps of his apartment building; he sat next to a ten-gallon aquarium. There was a sizable turtle in it. The young man called out: "Want a turtle." I remembered next that I heard: "You're, Sam Isaac." He added, "You're looking good."

Sam looked at him with one raised eyebrow and asked: "How do you know my name?" It turned out that he was one of the kids that the state worker served when he worked at State MH juveniles. It was ten-years ago, when he was thirteen. Immediately after he told me his name, I instantly remembered him. We shared a little conversation over the smoking of some marijuana in my apartment. Of course, if he was thirteen-years-of-age, now he was 22 years-old. Sam thought about his introduction to cannabis through Glenda.

Sam should've never smoked or given it to him the way Glenda did all those years ago, he uttered. Sam felt that it was remarkable to see the young man. Firstly, he looked nothing like he did as a young teenager. It was funny because the image in Sam's mind, at that time, pictured the youngling as a younger. So, as he sat in front of him it was a strange feeling to know their short history. They talked about his life. Sam knew the circumstances of how and why the youngster entered the State's residential, behavioral program. He battled with life just like everybody did.

These were good times. Sam was in good physical and mental shape. Marijuana was back in his life and he thanked God, because the cluster headaches never left me. The plant was made by Mother Nature. It helped Sam cope with agony. He stopped smoking cigarettes, months ago, and replaced it with cannabis. The plant, as indicated before, helped him. Not everybody who had cluster headaches found that cannabis helped the condition. In one study, only twenty-five percent found it helped. On the other end of the spectrum there were twenty-five percent who reported that it made the headaches worse for them. While the majority of cluster headache people, fifty percent, said that it made no difference at all. It didn't help them. But it didn't hurt. The pain went on. Sam used what worked, the cannabis, because he finally found a steady supplier. He was the first person that he bought it from on a consistent basis. Every time he needed it he was there. It allowed him to fight the torture. Sam started to turn the tables, and eventually, he gained the upper hand over them. He still got the headaches, but he fought them; it was war, and he was winning for once.

Malefic, however, had new plans for him. The State had lifted its hiring-freeze. Soon after, Sam was hired but this time by another division within the State MH System. He became a psychiatric caseworker. He was given a caseload of chronically mentally ill adults who he worked with. Sam helped them with all their business. Landlord problems, social security matters, trouble at the bank, etc. But he also presented, to the clients, the States MH psychosocial rehabilitation program. He taught adults in groups. It was life skills training, and he added his little shtick, from the classroom, as he implemented their program. Sam learned from the program that he taught. They were basic common-sense topics: Socialization, communication, coping skills, etc. Eventually, he finished working at that clinic. The collected data indicated that Malefic had transitioned him again. This time it was an assignment at another clinic. He performed the same duties but, only weeks after he arrived, he ruined it or he should've said that Malefic ruined it.

He had an episode that never happened to me before; he blew up. There were no clients at this brand-new clinic he was assigned to. It was brand new. They weren't fully staffed yet. One day Sam was seated at the front desk, and he was bored. He recalled, later, that he twiddled with a paperclip. During it the M-workers acted. It was something that he did and said to a coworker. She told me that she "hated the classical music" that I put on in the waiting room. I bolted out of my chair, and I told her that she "hated everything," and Sam stormed back to his office. The next day, when he was told that he was being disciplined for it. For the first time in his life and in his MH career, he really lost it and I quit.

Disturbed, Sam frantically went into his office and took down every drawing that the kids in the elementary schools had drawn for him for a present. Sam was caked into his sickness. He threw the gifts out when he got home he was so mad. They were tools that he used. He had them tacked up all over the wall space, so when he met with clients for individual one on one psycho-social rehabilitation sessions he found they worked because they set the right tone. He cherished all the drawings very much. He never asked for them. In those two-years, he substituted, which followed the "we hate you," message, he turned it around. He received more than a dozen drawings from children at different schools from different grades and classes. They personalized them and presented them to me. They thanked me, all in their own way, for being their substitute teacher that day.

Back when the cluster headaches started, the Veterans Administration (VA), tried everything modern medicine developed to fight it. None of it worked on Sam. He was, frequently, absent during his last year with the State in their MH system. The cluster headaches assaulted him each night; it was bad, and it happened so frequently that he said that he wanted to die. He quickly deteriorated, mentally. His illness kept him away so often that he forfeited pay. He had used up all his sick leave. He fell into a deep depression. In the last few months of his employment, his illness was so profound that he didn't shower. He had nothing to fight the cluster headaches with. He had a sick mind, in addition, but he was never connected to any MH services; he just worked at one.

They were simple words that carried a lot of weight. With his name "Mr. I."on the board, and all the students seated, he began: "Everybody has a good side to them and a bad side, and when you come to school you need to show your good side. You need to show it to your teacher. You need to show it to your fellow classmates, and you need to show it to yourself. Because you need to be aware that it's there, because your good side is a very important part of you, and you need to bring it out and use it!" I went on with their attention glued on me: "When we're at home our brothers and sisters, or someone shows us their bad sides, and we turn right around, and show them ours. It's an automatic reflex," Sam explained and demonstrated, "just like when the doctor hits your knee with a little rubber hammer your leg will always pop up. But you're not at home, you're at school, and so you've got to act differently. He continued: "What do you think that your mom and dad would do if they went to work, and they were silly and goofy, or they were mean or mad. What do you think would happen to them if they did that? The answer always came back: "They'd be fired." Sam would agree with them and then added -- so, school is a very important place. And when we are in public, which means that we're not at home. This is your job, and you'll have this job for many years, and then you'll have a grown-up job just like a grown-up. So, when you come to school, show your good side: "when we show our good side, good things happen to us. When we show our bad side, bad things happen. So, when you find yourself in an important place, it's important to show your best. Never your worst."

Chapter 4

Sam packed up his car, again, and he drove from Pennsylvania to California. He managed to settle all his startup needs for a bed and recliner - he did it just like I always did, a studio apartment, a bed and recliner. Once again, he unloaded the car. As he did it some men talked nearby. One said that he was a veteran. At that time, Sam had the energy of a broken-down lawn mower. He felt dragged down, as his possessions entered his latest dwelling. In and out he went until the conversation between the two men, Sam noticed, had stopped. Mindlessly, he approached the veteran, and he told the guy that he was a veteran and that he was wondering where a veteran would go in the town to get help. He asked me: What kind of help? Sam said that he was sick and physically exhausted.

That action had been forethought. He was, once again, controlled by Malefic. The M-workers had him on automatic pilot.

The veteran knew just what to do, since he had been mentally ill and homeless before. The VA had helped the Viet Nam vet. They paid his rent when he moved into the studio apartment next to Sam. The next day a veteran's outreach worker met with Sam. Jack, the worker, was very tall and likable. After he came to Sam's apartment that day he placed his dog in a dog-hotel, because once he interviewed Sam and completed his documentation, he drove Sam to Los Angeles. The soldier spent two-weeks at a VA hospital in a locked MH unit. He was there voluntarily, but others were not. Sam had, of course, worked at one, but he had never been a patient in one. To me it made a difference. He felt comfortable there. But he told nobody why. Days passed and he felt the depression lift. "It was quite wonderful." He recuperated nicely. It took a year, but he dropped all the excess weight, because of water retention (excess salt) and most importantly, mentally, he felt much better. Hewas on an antidepressant, and cluster headaches left him alone for that year.

The new job required all M-workers to scramble, and it couldn't have been timed better, Sam realized later. This job required a physical and a drug test. He was in shape for both. There had been no marijuana in his system ever since he returned from the hospital a year ago. He had no need for it.

He passed the tests and was hired. Later, he still took antidepressants. But the cluster headaches returned. When it happened, it was bad. He knew just what to do. He obtained medical marijuana, it was before recreational legalization, and he self-medicated. It battled the pain. Sam took a deep hit, and he held it in as he thought: "Take that you mother fucker!" He could feel the battle going on. It was like a plumber's snake. It unclogged the congestion up the nostril. It took several hits until he turned the corner, and it went away. Once, Sam was in Amsterdam, courtesy, of all people, Glenda. She had invited him, Frank and Lily to join her as she was on assignment in Paris. Sam went at her expense. The cluster headaches in France never relented. Once, she hired a tour bus. It took us to sights all over gay-Paree. As the bus rolled by Parisians a cluster headache started. It got so bad it brought him to tears, which it had done before. She remembered that he looked right into Glenda's face because I knew that my eye appeared as if it had been punched several times. I screamed in agony: "YOU SEE!" She had no sympathy or empathy in her eyes because she hated her brother, and she liked seeing him suffer.

Sam spent three days in the city of canals. Its history never escaped him but he was there for the marijuana. Once purchased he bought a pipe. He went back to his hotel room and smoked. When he smoked, in those years, he always smoked a cigarette afterwards. He crushed the butt into an empty ashtray, laid down, and I fell asleep. Hours later, however, he awakened with a terrible cluster attack. Sam grabbed the pipe and marijuana and went to the darkened bathroom. Any light agitated the pain even more and it was daytime. In the darkness he sat on the toilet seat. The pain roared like a lion that had been hit by a snap of the whip. Sam's hands trembled as he stuffed the cannabis into the pipe. He shielded my tortured eye from the brightness of the flame. He deeply inhaled, something he couldn't do, if he didn't have a cluster headache, and he just wanted to get high. He held the medicine from God, and he sniffed it a few times to make the medicine go further up the sinus passage that was clogged.

On that day, he experienced a miracle. The power of cannabis broke through the clog immediately. Woosh, it stopped. It took only seconds. That time had freed Sam from its grip on his brain and the dagger in his eye. To me it was a miracle. He stayed high while he was there. He walked through the city streets. Once, he stepped off a street curb. A few seconds went by before a quiet electric streetcar should've smacked right into me. Sam was in its path as he stepped onto the street. He wasn't injured or killed, and he believed if that was on the menu that day, it would have happened. Decades later he thanked Malefic and the M-team for the marijuana experience that he had there. Sam was spared, that time, from the evil clutches of the suicide headache.

After that he just used cannabis. The job that he was hired for was in Sacramento. It was a non-profit organization. It had many treatment facilities located throughout the United States.

Sam was hired into a new program; it started, only, a year ago. It was a day program for chronically mentally ill adults. The program required, though, a SMI diagnosis with psychosis.

He was hired as a psychosocial rehabilitation specialist at a program called Options. The program was housed in an old MH unit of a psychiatric hospital that was no longer there. The rest of the building housed the county's social service offices. Option's area had two padded seclusion rooms, which housed file cabinets. It also had a nurse's station as its headquarters. The station sat between eight rooms. They housed the patients in the old psych-ward. Now, those rooms were all offices. A secretary sat at the helm in the nurse's station. The psychiatric nurse was also a charge nurse in that area. She was a woman born and bred in the country of Buddha, India. She always dressed in traditional Indian garments. She never wore anything else. We, also, had two social workers Sandy and Mark. There was a psychiatrist, Doctor Chavez, who came twice a week to see people. But the program had an odd executive director. His name was Bill. His oddity was that he was the administrator. He never led a MH program before. Besides that, frankly, Sam thought he was weird. Once, Sam guided client's into a group room. It was empty and they sat down and started the group. Two minutes went by and suddenly those in attendance heard a toilet in action; it was loud. The sound came from the executive director's private bathroom. It seemed that they came in and started while Bill sat on the throne. Bill always reads the newspaper and reads. Sam was aware of Bill's routine because he cleaned up for him, and stocked each of the four bathrooms, that was his one-chore every day, and Bill's restroom was one of them. That day's print always side-saddled the commode. Sam knew because he threw it out Monday through Friday. After the group Bill called Sam to his office, and he looked like he was determined to find out why me and my client's were in their area. Sam told him that he had no idea who was in his restroom. The door to it was closed, and Sam didn't have a habit of knocking on it to check if Bill or anyone was in there. That's when Bill realized that he didn't like Sam. Bill hired him, so he was forever in his debt. Bill never harmed Sam in his mind's eye even though the guy tried.

Sam shared an office with another PSR worker, Ellena. She was very likable and giddy. Sam and Ellena both ran separate psychosocial rehabilitation groups twice per day. For the rest of their time, they provided case management services. Just like he did when he was a psychiatric caseworker. People, especially those with chronic mental illness, had a lot of case management needs, and Sam did his best to serve them. He performed one good deed after another. In fact, he performed so many good deeds during his MH education, that he felt, years later, it offset his teenage criminality, which would have surely continued if Malefic had not pulled the plug on it.

On average twenty SMI people from the community spent their day at the Meyer's Club. One or two individuals were homeless and came to us by day, and by night one or two went back to the shelters. Others came to the charity as referrals. They lived all over the county, and one of Sam's jobs was to transport people. He rarely picked anybody up, but he routinely drove them home in a fifteen-passenger van after the program closed for the day. Of all the positions that Sam held, in so many other capacities in the field, this assignment was the best because he was filled with knowledge. Thoughts presented themselves to him at all hours of the day and night. The typist wrote down each thought on scratch paper. Every day, there was more. Sam kept the notes in a big plastic bag. Prior to his employment, he wrote a book. He used the knowledge that he learned in the book at his new job. The words that Sam had to offer were not his. He never took credit for another's work, which Bill did to him once. but, frankly, Sam never knew where it came from. The non-religious example of a man never was caught reading anything about it. He never watched or listened to anything either. And he never talked about it with anyone. Sam, honestly, never knew of Malefic in those days. The magical force worked in the right orbit, but it was never focused on Malefic. Nobody did. Malefic returned to me for some reason. Through all those years, Sam never processed his criminality, even though he was aware of it. Having an awareness that something was wrong. It still bothered him a great deal, because he wanted to know. What does all this mean? And why was the lawbreaker blinded by Malefic, for half a century, until the knowledge was revealed, and then processed? Sam never knew exactly what occurred. It was quite remarkable because throughout his whole life he lived and worked in a MH arena. It stayed with him every hour that he remained awake. The answers, to his questions, were right in front of him the whole time. The likable dude knew the different diagnostic terms. SMI people were diagnosed with it in the process. But Sam never held a clinical position, and, so, he never knew the symptoms for being diagnosed with Bipolar. Or Sam never knew about personality disorders symptoms of things like APD or ASPD. The man never knew the headlines of diagnosis i.e. what is schizophrenia, but, never once, in all my years of service did he just open a book to read about what the criteria were for a particular diagnosis. Sam never bothered to look. He had no reason to do it.. It wasn't part of his work. Why people were diagnosed with this or that wasn't relevant to what he did. Sam had a job, and he did it. As for Tony, it never mattered. Sam's words shattered upon the wooden deck of the summer cabin that they all shared. Sam saw a psychiatrist at the VA, and he was placed on different medications.

It wasn't until Sam's twilight years that it was finally revealed to the man. Malefic gave Sam a taste of himself, again. Sam was deceived for decades. If Sam knew the truth, at any time, his MH career would've ended. But because he learned later, that he hadn't even come out of the womb, and he was already damned.

Sam wanted to know who he was. The competent MH employee, the substitute teacher, the MH client, the patient, or the thief? Why was he the way he was? He never cried loneliness because it was not that. Sam just wanted to befriend others for two things – sex and marijuana. If people he knew weren't in either category, he would be friendly and he helped them if he could. But she never connected socially. He never spent time with regular people, especially after work. Sam went home to his lazy little dog back then, and he simply stayed home alone. Six-and-one-half decades went by before the puzzle, finally and fully, presented itself. Sam had to put it together. He solved it, over a period of time, but really, it did not take very long.

Sam recalled strong memories. A single moment, forty-five years ago, still burned brightly inside his being, just like they all did. The romantic couple on the television flashed him back to when he stood on an escalator going up. He was in a department store, and he looked up in front of himself and there was a heterosexual couple. They held hands. The strong visual memory was always accompanied by equally strong audio. It was an old *Moody Blues* song. The tune and a single lyric played in his mind. *Gazing at people, some hand-in-hand, just what I'm going through they can't understand.* But Sam understood, and it changed everything for him.

No longer was his MH education just about the good side. A flow of wisdom warmed Sam's eyes that night. It came one piece at a time. He compiled the pieces, and along with his good side, shtick, and the psychosocial rehabilitation information, it turned out good. The younger Isaac was successful in the short run. SMI people smiled, and some told him that they liked being at the program. Some, Sam can recall, told him that they felt good when they were at the club.. Folks got involved in the different groups. People/s attitudes were very positive. People were genuinely kind. The seeded information led to one thing: the growth of goodness.

The leadership of the program, including the psychiatrist, wanted to know just what the MH worker was doing. They interviewed clients. They asked them what they've learned in Sam's group. They wanted to see some of the hand-out materials. They questioned his integrity. None of the leadership ever sat in one of his groups, which they were welcomed to do. But when Bill found out what Sam taught he just told him that he had to stop using acronyms. That was it. They didn't question Sam about the content of the philosophy. If they did, he would have told them; it was knowledge passed down to me, for me to pass down to others.

But it wasn't all roses. Sam had his critics. He recalled there were two program members who stopped coming to his group in his second year. They were, usually, at the program for the entire day, but they never came into Sam's groups anymore. One of them said that the teacher talked too much. That the client hardly ever got time to say anything. Sam explained that he taught behavioral skills. It wasn't a free-for-all discussion group. It was structured, well, sort of. His bag of notes came out. There must have been a hundred little notes. Everyday, he reached in and pulled out one and talked about whatever topic it covered. However, Sam accepted the criticism, because with Sam, everybody has to be okay with whatever he was doing, so he made changes. He still taught behavioral skills but he shortened his presentations. It opened discussion for the last fifteen-minutes of the hour. But those two guys never showed up to the group regardless but they were the first to challenge Sam in his career.

For the first time in Sam's career someone stood up and challenged him when it came to his work with chronically mentally ill adults. They questioned his role as a leader of the psychosocial rehabilitation groups that he facilitated. There were other clients who may have felt that way but Sam always saw himself as a leader that he was in command and that he was in charge. The groups continued under his stewardship because whatever he was doing he was doing it right. Other clients who came forward spoke a different language and expressed that Sam was someone worth listening to and they supported him by attending his groups. But Sam knew that something was wrong with him ever since he walked across the threshold of the

Meyer's Club. That's when he started getting help for his mental health, something he would not be made completely aware of until the non-hero reached a certain point and it would be revealed to him.

Sam was in the teacher's

The mental health employee conducted himself as someone who was doing something very important. One critic said that Sam always acted as if he was in charge and he believed that he was right about everything or that he could create something that people would say that he's right. He would wiggle his way out of whatever word salad that he was serving. So not everybody saw eye to eye with him but Sam was the leader, that is why he was successful. It was because of his ability to think only of himself in that spot. He dominated that spot. He knew and understood that that spot was his leadership. To all the people Sam served while in Mental Health he was always looked upon as a counselor/advisor. Someone who looked in charge and acted accordingly. The leader was Sam and his followers were the people he served. Those two group members who believed Sam was a problem were being challenged because Sam believed, and acted without hesitation, that he was in control while he worked in mental health and he acted like it as well, and under Sam's rules the maker of magic was doing nothing more than spreading goodness amongst his clan.

The county started a new housing development for the homeless. To those who met the criteria it meant they received a new, one-bedroom, apartment. It was stocked with everything: furniture, plates, silverware, glasses, a coffee maker, sheets, pillowcases, cleaning supplies, even toilet paper. Two clients in the Option's program met the criteria. Applications were completed, and Sam helped one client as he moved into his new home. Bill loved the story. The company had a monthly newsletter. Bill decided that he wanted Sam to take photographs of the man at his new home. Bill, also, wanted Sam to write a story about it. Bill planned to send it to the company's newsletter for publication. So, Sam wrote it effortlessly. Weeks went by and one day, the new newsletter was issued. Every word of it made it into ink, except for who wrote it. Sam's name was omitted and Bill's name replaced it. On the front page of it was one of the pictures that the photographer took that day as well. Along with it was the story. Bill sent an email to each of us; it stated that Sam deserved all the credit.

Malefic, Sam learned later, ordered another transition for him after two years at that job. This time instead of Sam having another crisis; it was Dad instead. His last one. The good son was on medical family sick-leave for six-weeks. He stayed at his father's place, and he visited him for a few hours every day. Sam realized, much later, that he was, finally, being processed out of the MH field. Malefic played with Sam first. He was sent through hell to get to where he felt safe, happy and a ton of energy. Meanwhile, the desire to find other MH jobs entered his consciousness.

Sam thought about going back to work for the State. He completed an application. He drove eight-hours round trip to the interview. The supervisors liked what Sam said, but, when all was said and done, they never hired him. Someone in State personnel got wind that Sam had reapplied for another position and, once again, it was for a MH position with the State. It appeared; however, that Isaac's last "I quit" caused the word to get out: State jobs were now closed to him.

Soon after, Eric called him. He needed his son's help. He was not well, he said, and he lived five-hours away, and because, at age eighty, he was Sam's father, the kid used his sick leave and went to him. The hospital had Eric tied to a machine for six-weeks, and the day his insurance ran out they shipped him to a hospice. He died alone; Sam didn't know that he was transported there. Malefic spared Sam from going to his funeral as well. Because when Sam went back to California, his energy was zapped! He couldn't drive five-hours or even five-minutes. Eric's sister, a great aunt, Nelly, Frank and Pat flew in from the east coast. They held a little ceremony for Eric at the Veterans' cemetery, where his ashes were interred.

If Malefic ever shared any secrets, it was now. It was a crazy path. When Sam returned from his father's ordeal, Bill was super pissed at his employee. He wrote Sam up for taking off for six-weeks, and Bill said: "That I never called in." Sam knew, when he left, that he took family sick leave so that he could be with his dad. Besides, Bill gave Sam the paperwork and the doctor signed it; he approved Sam's absence. But Bill went ahead with the admonishment anyway. He never questioned him. Like Sam said, Bill could do no harm.

He thought it was because the company's personnel director told Bill that he was in violation of the civil rights act ergo, he discriminated against Sam, and he could have initiated a civil-rights complaint with the Federal Civil Rights Division. Sam believed that he would have won and he told Bill, according to Malefic. Sam never did anything about it otherwise. Even so, he was out-the-door two weeks later when he returned to California.

Malefic had the M-team in action. Malefic instructed M-watchers to ensure Sam's quick departure, just as before in the navy. M-workers used a staff meeting. Malefic delivered the means necessary for Bill to escort him off the property, because he was fired on the spot. Malefic knew Sam's weaknesses. M-planners were familiar too and knew what was deep inside of him. What he expected didn't help matters.

It had been years since he had sex. Sam gave up on his attempts at socializing. He was never able to. He never experienced love because he never had a sexual experience with anyone while he worked at the program. At a lull in the staff meeting Ellen approached Sam and she told him that one of the clients, Carlton, "really likes you." There were no more words uttered, and it didn't matter. Malefic triggered the rock. It was the revelation that led Sam into action. The day before Sam was fired, he took people home from the program out for lunch. He planned it so that the client and he were the last two people in the van. Sam's impulsivity awakened the M-workers who shot the hormone of desire into him. Sam told the client, who liked him too, that he had strong feelings for him. A power overwhelmed Sam with feelings that he never had before. There was no sex, he gave Sam a kiss on the cheek when he dropped him off. Of course, he later realized what Sam did was a complete violation of the rules. But he was blinded to the consequences at the time. When he came to work the next day, he conducted his morning group. There were new program participants; they were first timers and Sam decided that he wanted to present the totality of the information to them.

Basically, the information came from Malefic and it was about people's self. The information laid out was to build an understanding of the soul and self. Sam talked about the importance of having: self-awareness, self-respect, self-esteem, self-confidence and self-kindness. This acronym was called ARECK. The next stage's acronym was RFGLUCK, which stood for: Respect, friendship, goodness, love, understanding, compassion and kindness; towards self and others. Sam presented a variety of information which included the good-side information from when he was a substitute teacher, and, most importantly, about how the self and soul must be "united." Sam asked the clients to recall a saying, which stemmed from World War I: The words *United We Stand, Divided We Fall* emphasized how critical and important it was to show respect for mankind's vehicle of life. Sam emphasized the word *self* because he understood that people with mental illness, especially, serious mental illness, cared very little for themselves. The teacher wanted to introduce the students to themselves. Everybody in the group understood when someone said: "I need to find myself." The instigator of truth thought and said: *Today, you found it.* Treat the self as you would want others to treat it. Regarding self, the way he explained it: Soul and self-come together to create the individual person. And, after people's journey through life. After the soul and self separate and self was buried into the ground, and soul returned from whence it came.

It was to be Sam's final performance. At the end of the group one new participant popped out of his seat. He approached the facilitator and stuck out his hand. Sam remembered that he said: "That was great." The group leader was always touched when those kinds of moments happened, and it helped with what was to be, otherwise, a gloomy day.

So, Sam was out of work. Later, he realized all these events came courtesy of Malefic. He left California and moved in with Ellen, in Las Vegas. He had money to support himself for at least six-months. Once, he attempted to return to the non-profits in the MH field. He drove a six-hour round trip back to California. The applicant interviewed in front of three people. Everything went fine until they got into specifics. Sam talked about his mental health experience. He spoke about the types of behaviors and how he handled certain matters. The questioner asked him something like: "What would you do if you had a group of chronically mentally ill adults who had no coping skills?"

Sam thought for a few seconds and then he spoke about what he did, and everything was going fine up to that point. At the conclusion of his answer, however, he said that client's felt better about themself and were more relaxed with themselves and with others, which was the feedback he received a number of times. The interviewee ended his answer: "Then I would sit back and watch all of the magic the words unleashed." The two other panelists never looked up at Sam until he said that. The questioner asked: "What magic is that?" Sam answered that it's the magic that occurred when people's self esteem improved. That is when they opened up and actually lived. The interviewer approached Sam and he patted him on the back and put his arm around his shoulder as they walked out of the office. Sam was never hired. He went back to Las Vegas, and after the money ran out, he applied for Social Security Disability. He never worked in the MH field again.

For thirty-years he was on the job day and night. He worked with client after client. He served patient after patient. Even though he was still tortured by cluster headaches, he deduced, much later, after all these years, that his MH education, courtesy of Malefic, had been completed.

Chapter 3

Manuel's tendency to quibble with every word that Lily uttered became a warning sign that her adoptive son built a resentment that led to severe friction between the two of them. Lily was never mean or mad; it just wasn't her way. As a teacher she captured her student's hearts with her words, tone and manner. Power wasn't important to Lily, but she gained it anyway because of the way she disarmed all that she encountered. Manuel's mental acuity told her that despite his background, before the age of four, in her mind, he flourished. She believed that she'd set him free from the maltreatment he experienced, and she provided him with all the love and attention he needed.

Before the boy reached ten, Lily had only one telltale sign that there was something wrong. It was when he was paddled at school. The boy never forgot it. Later, I thought that's when he tripped the wire.

Otherwise, he had a dream book childhood. He vacationed every summer with his mom. They both loved animated movies. They watched them together regularly, especially the Disney films. Their living room wall was filled with framed photos. My favorite picture of them was when they went to *Walt Disney World* in Florida. Lily was big on history, too. Especially America's. She took Manuel to visit many historical sites. They took a trip to Gettysburg, Pennsylvania. They stood on the historic battlefields and toured the museum. Next, they toured the nation's capital. Lily wanted Manuel to be happy and she loved him very much. But she wanted him informed. He learned and understood just what democracy was. She thought that he was too young and spared from the politics, so he never learned of the perversion perpetuated by Pliartrum against the Constitution, Democracy and against the American people. Lily knew if the extremist ever got their way it would be the Confederate States of America, again, something they attempted to install back in the mid-nineteenth Century. Lily fought hard for the blue side. She wrote a blog, which encouraged the Anti-Pliartrum Party, or otherwise known as the People Party. She wanted voters to nominate Pliartrum's nephew, Horace Pliartrum as the opposition leader to the Country Club Party.

"I wanted him as the nominee because he was an eminent psychiatrist who stood up to his uncle when he was elected and won the Oval Office." Lily believed the former president's nephew, Horace, had the chutzpah to stand up to his uncle and organized crime. Horace described his kin as a tyrant. He referred to him in his book: "As the deadliest threat to this democracy since the Civil War.

Lily wasn't all politics, however. She had friends. She had a life. She was generous with her time and money. She helped whenever and wherever she could. She wanted to instill those traits, along with strong moral values, steadfastness and ethos into Manuel.

The honeymoon lasted for years. The boy was loved, and he received everything he wanted with one exception that Sam remembered. He wanted to wear sneakers to his first day at kindergarten. Lily had bought a nice outfit and shoes to wear but the clothes didn't match the sneakers. Manuel didn't listen to reason, so Lily ordered him to take his sneakers off, and to put on the new shoes. The boy never let it go, she said. When he reached his adolescents, he wore nothing but sneakers, even when he wore a tie and jacket. He started to rebel in other ways as well. Lily said that he talked back. He took no advice from her. He defied her, constantly. She talked to him about it, and, sometimes, he listened. But it was all an act; deep down a cauldron boiled.

It was just one day that she stoked the fire and, possibly, paid a price for it. Manuel and Lily had another "fight." It started when he manipulated her for money, and he stole a credit card from her purse. He charged up three-thousand dollars as a runaway. He wined and dined and stayed at a fancy hotel for three-nights. When he came home his temper flared when confronted with what he did.

"He quickly escalated," she told Sam. His expression and words shifted from meekness, with more lies and excuses, and words like please, Mom – to fuck you, bitch. I don't give a fuck what you say. Manuel looked, and pointed his finger at Lily, like her son had been crossed, she said. There was a high level of vengefulness in his eyes. They pushed, shoved, and threw things at each other. Lily told me that he grabbed her arm and yanked at it with a sadistic look in his eyes. The bone snapped. She cried out in agony. She looked up and he yelled at her; "it's your fault!"

Suddenly, it was like he shifted gears. He melted like butter on a hot biscuit. His anger lifted. His eyes changed. He looked at her with compassion and remorse. He turned himself around quicker than an eggbeater. He drove her to the hospital. He cried and apologized all the way there and all the way back home. But, with Lily now in a cast she believed that he must face consequences. She unfolded her case at the kitchen table. In a cast, she explained that he needed to help himself;

it was time for him to grow-up. Apparently, sometime ago, he stopped taking antidepressants, and he used marijuana. She knew it but she was blinded to do anything about it. Malefic, again. Any substance abuse fueled his fire, which Lily understood. It was both genetic and environmental. He was born into it. Before the age of four he lived in hell. She lifted him out of it for the remainder of his childhood with the help of love and psychotropic medications. But it was just a *Band-Aid* on a gaping wound. Lily never learned of his behavior in high school. "He was a nice guy," someone said from his school, "until you crossed him." Lily did more than that, she threw him out and told him that he could not come back until he stopped the marijuana and started taking his antidepressants again. He stayed with friends only two weeks before it was accomplished.

However, it interested Sam to read amongst her documents that she had a file about our Uncle Stu, who was Sam's mother's brother. The shifty uncle had quite an entanglement with Lily over her comment about Pliartrum. She shared the comment she wrote about the president with her elder uncle. After he read it the fact that Uncle Stu was pro-Pliartrum didn't go unnoticed. With poison in his pen he wrote back with an angry response, the last line of which was threatening. "I wish you all the best." Lily wrote that her uncle's words sounded like a mob send-off.

Chapter 4

Sam was informed that Glenda held Dorothy's hand when she took her last breath. Lilly and Frank stood by her side before her expiration as well and Pat reported to Sam that Lily fainted. When Dorothy died Sam was not by her side. He was at Frank's Patriot Park Home. He moved in, once again – Sam traveling again. The family really grieved over Dorothy, Sam did not. The other siblings spoke of their beloved mother who, sadly, had "passed away." Sam was much more direct; he just said: "She died."

The cold weather met with gusty winds; it shook the naked trees as it rained. There were one-hundred-thirty-nine friends and family who came to the solemn affair. They each signed the book and paid their respects. The cemetery was large. There was row after row of headstones. It was cold inside the building that housed Dorothy's casket. There were a lot of benches. A sizable red carpet separated them down the middle. There was no comfort for anyone. Each person sat on a hard wooden bench. Inside were the many people who knew Dorothy during her lifetime. They were packed inside like sardines. In the front rows family members were split. On one side it was me, Lily, Manuel. Across the aisle was Glenda, Frank and Pat. Sam was in the poorest physical and mental shape that he had experienced throughout his MH education. To add insult to injury, Pat told Sam that he smelled. He had showered and changed his underpants before he came after a week of doing neither.

The ceremony started and the Rabbi entered. Sam should've never known there were one-hundred-thirty-nine people behind him because, suddenly, he heard a pin drop. The serious man of faith spoke about Dorothy and her accomplishments. He noted that she had been a lifetime member of the synagogue. That she was a good woman. He added that she was a hard worker and a good mother.

Next, Glenda stood up graciously. She moved to the lectern. She had on her serious PROX NEWS expression and used her serious tone of voice, as she delivered her prepared remarks. She said that Dorothy was an angel and that she was the best mother a person, like her, could ever have. Next, Lily spoke. She recapped how Dorothy struggled as she raised the children alone. Sam never rose that day to speak. He never spoke a word, verbally, during the entire affair. Non-verbally, however, he spoke volumes. The casket was guided down the red carpet and rolled outside to the burial plot. The Religious Leader followed it, and the family was behind them with their heads lowered. Everyone followed the family outside.

The dreary day never went away. A cold rain fell and the wind was brisk. A large green tent housed the open six-foot deep grave with a mound of red earth adjoined to it. On the other side, six wooden folding chairs were reserved for the family. Glenda sat at one end, Sam sat at the other. Everybody looked somber. The comfortability level was high for the attendees. The cold temperature made the wind and rain even more wicked and unbearable. As people took shelter under the awning and beneath their umbrellas, they all waited silently for the man of God to fall silent. The mound of earth had a silver spade in it. The funeral leader held out the spade and gestured for people to come forward and pay their respect. First, however, he shoveled a spade with a symbolic amount of dirt into the hole.

Mindlessly, before a soul moved forward to take the tool, Sam popped out of his seat. He grabbed the shovel from the Rabbi's hand and briskly shoveled spade after spade full of red earth, back into its hole. The total amount that he transferred were five shovels full; it covered her entire casket. Sam would have kept going, mindlessly, but someone tapped him on the shoulder to stop, which he did, and he handed the spade to the person, and he returned to his seat avoiding eye contact with everyone.

As for Dorothy and Sam's relationship, their estrangement began soon after Eric ran off with Ellen. There were 3 incidents that best described why there wasn't any positive emotional attachment, and why, years later, Sam felt that, at age 10, Dorothy stopped loving him, and he stopped loving her. The night was hot and humid. There was no breeze. The air was so still that when Sam's young eyes looked out the window even the giant weeping-willow tree's branches in the backyard never swayed. The air was so still that the sounds Sam heard at that moment came through strong and clear. It was his mother. She was downstairs. There was a man with her. It was a voice Sam recognized from when the family went to the community pool during weekends in the summer.

The sun scorched the sidewalk that day. Sam's little feet, only a decade old, scuttled quickly across the concrete with a note in his hand. Dorothy sent Sam to deliver a note to the lifeguard, and she told her son that it was very important to her.

The man in the chair sat very high above the glistening Olympic-sized pool that was filled with people. As the water splashed and kids screamed, intermittently, as they played, the lifeguard's naked torso suddenly popped up as he clutched the whistle from around his neck. He inhaled and he let out a whistle-blow that turned every head in the pool. As he stood on his lifeguard chair, high above, he bellowed to some kids who were rough housing in the water. Sam stood at the foot of the towering seat and looked up at him. The worker sat back down, and Sam called out to him. It was noisy, but he heard Sam. He told the adult that he had a note for him from his mom. He reached down and took it. Sam never knew what the note was about until that night when he heard them downstairs. It sounded like Dorothy hurt herself. Her voice sounded distressed as she said "it hurts."Then the boy heard the lifeguard tell her: "It's okay. I'm going to take it nice and easy. It's okay. Just very slow. Mm mM-does that feel good. Sam cringed as his mother's moaning bothered him greatly. As he got back in bed he listened intently to every word and every sound.

It was Sam's first exposure to sex, although it was just audio. Perhaps if it were visual, it may have disturbed him more. Nevertheless, it must have impacted him in a negative way because he got into big trouble. Not the kind that gets you spanked but the kind that brings on shame from another. In this case it was Dorothy and Glenda.

They were seated on the couch side-by-side one day soon after. Dorothy bellowed Sam's full name so loud that it startled him as he lay on his stomach with his feet up in the air, a pencil in his hand, and a notebook that he was writing in. The wooden floor creaked as he got to the head of the stairs and slowly made my way down. As he clutched the wooden railing the steps creaked even louder than the floor above. When he got to the base of the stairs he turned and saw them. What they said made Sam very uncomfortable. Sam had always been able to say what happened to himself, but he never understood why it happened. Dorothy's tone was harsh. As she yelled, Sam looked at Glenda who, he later thought, looked stimulated by it in some queer way. Sam was accused of touching Frank's genitals. In fact, he was shamed for kissing his penis once. At the age of 5, Frank turned to Glenda, and she told Dorothy. He thought that was the day that she stopped loving him because, years later, when he looked back and started to process all this kind of stuff in his life, he remembered that after that he had little to no frills in those days. He did go to that summer camp where he, unfortunately, met Tony. Was it Malefic, he wondered years later. Was Tony meant to come into Sam's life to teach him a lesson, he wondered years later?

The luncheon that followed Dorothy's funeral brought everyone together again. Their mother lived in a townhouse in a development. The downstairs was full of people. Sam walked upstairs and sat in an overstuffed chair. He was physically and mentally exhausted. He never knew it but Malefic, at last, had broken me. I was present for those that gathered to mourn that day. But I never grieved, not even for a second. Plans were set in the late afternoon for dinner that evening. It was Sam, Uncle Stu, Glenda, Lily, Manuel, Pat and Frank. People came by day and night as the family just sat there, on little chairs for seven-days. A mountain of food arrived. Sam answered the door once, and a neighbor brought us a lemon bundt cake. He never liked lemon bundt cakes. But Sam's eyes widened anyway as his dinky eyebrows raised in astonishment. He made an "ooh" sound to her. It was another one of his attempts to get attention and to please someone.

The meal that night consisted of an array of leftovers from the luncheon earlier in the day. Afterwards it was Glenda's turn to take center stage. She pulled out the family photo albums and she went through each page. Lily got up and went into the kitchen as Glenda continued. She had a story for every photo. There was a black and white photo of me when Sam was seven. He had a huge booger coming out of his nose. Another one was of Dorothy. Their mother stood outside, in front of a clothesline filled with white sheets. Glenda pointed out that she was nine-months pregnant with Sam. And then she said: "Look at that serious expression on her face," and then she looked at Sam with sad puppy dog eyes. She acted gleeful and giddy as if she'd never seen any of the photos before.

Afterwards, Lily cleared the table; Pat helped her. Manuel sat in the living room and watched television as Sam listened to Uncle Stu and Glenda. They talked about Dorothy, and they reminisced about people they once knew and who had died. It went on. They enjoyed their after-meal coffee. Maybe it was Sam's fault. He asked Glenda where her boyfriend Pliartrum, Junior was. She looked at Sam like it's none of your fucking business. But it moved the ball into that territory. The family argued. Our warm family expressions shifted to cold political stares. Everyone acted as if they were glued to their favorite news channels and they had just received word that their political foes crossed the line, again. But this time they went too far. Lily, who rinsed and loaded the dishwasher, stood in the doorway between the two rooms. She dried her hands with a dish towel.

She asked: "What in the hell is going on out here? Have you people lost your minds?"

Glenda took the bait. She offered her smart aleck expression as she filled our minds with the gut wrenching reports about the People Party. She stood for all the craziness. She had gobbledygook about toasters, banana cream pies, and *"I Love Lucy,"* who she described as a woman who brought no femininity to her role. "You could tell she didn't give a hoot about the way she looked and dressed. I thought that she was too drab." In her mind, according to Sam, it was not *"I Love Lucy,"* it was: "Lesbians Love Lucy."

There was conflict everywhere. M-watchers relayed all the data up the chain. Glenda declared war. Lilly's comments hit a homerun and Uncle Stu stared at her with contempt when the subject of religion arose.

Lily responded to Glenda's last utterance that God answered people's prayers. "So, you think that God has the time to pay attention to every soul on the planet?" "And what about Jesus, Mohammed and Buddha," she asked.

Uncle Stu shot all of us down. He pointed his finger at Lily who had just sat back down. He said earnestly, "We're going to wipe you sons-of-bitches out."

If Uncle Stu had his way, Americans believed only in Pliartrum. The Rule of Law and democracy was denounced, and a new oligarchical system, like Russia, emerged. The entire Federal Government would be privatized. Even our militaries would be in private hands. They planned a purge. In their minds they've already swelled the ranks of Federal employees with "their people," but "there's more to be done," according to Glenda. "The takeover started on January 6, 2021, just ten-months ago." Pliartrum was out of Office by then. But now it's crazy according to Malefic. Pliartrum's War on America, however, went into action the second he left the nation's capital and then returned to it. He had people in place to monitor the internet, particularly YouTube, for anything which was subversive to him. If there was something outrageous then the former president was made aware of it. That's how he saw Lily's YouTube comment.

Lily told Frank that he abandoned the truth when he supported Pliartrum. "He's killing this country," she said, long before *J6*. It began innocently. My brother's admiration for the loudmouth thug. "He watched his television show every week," Pat told me. He once explained, to me, before the hostility and *J6*, that Pliartrum recharged him. He told me that he felt powerful feelings that he never had before. He turned on his favorite newscast, each night, which was anchored by his favorite family member. PROX News had a grip on Frank's testicles even before Pliartrum entered the Oval Office. He watched Glenda and absorbed every talking point. With his heightened cynicism he shouted words of encouragement at her on the television, especially when she had a segment on the president's son, according to Pat. Demonization became a hobby for Frank. He thought people should help themselves. I asked him: "What's wrong with the government helping people in need?" He shot back like a Pliartrum stooge: "What do you want me to do about it?"

In 2016, I lived in another State, but I kept in contact with Frank, all through Pliartrum's first term in office. To Frank and his core cohorts, the fantastic five, which was what I called them, it all started out like one-big-joke. Frank loved the way Pliartrum pushed back at the press. Frank hated the legitimate press. He disliked it because Pliartrum did. He was one-hundred percent Glenda and PROX News, who he deemed "the only source for truth." A spell was casted over him. Overnight, it seemed, he transformed himself. He was no longer the tall skinny kid without a care in the world. He never was political before Pliartrum, but he signed up right away to be a Pliartrum canvasser for the president. He attended meetings and socialized a great deal. The main course in this dastardly meal was hatred towards every Federal Institution which enforced laws. Hatred for Blacks and illegal immigrants, gays, lesbians and transgender. I never heard a discouraging word out of Frank about hating Jews. But I told him, his association with Pliartrum and his people, said a lot about him in that department. In the early part of Pliartrum's term we'd talk for an hour.

He presented his talking points, and I presented mine. We were civil. We let each other talk. We said nice things to each other in between all the Pliartrum talk. But, as the years passed, we talked less. And when we did talk there were fireworks. His tone was loud; it never was before. He was smitten with Pliartrum.

Later, he took on a dedication to the former president that impacted his wife and children. Pat went to the bottle more. Sarah went to her friend's house. It was all to drown out Frank's radicalism.

On weekends it was nothing but Pliartrum. From 2017 when Pliartrum took Office, to 2018, Frank was with his "group," Keith, Don, Catch and Sammy. The fivesome fed off each other with their beer bottles in hand at the bar in the basement. Each week they gathered to talk about Pliartrum and about all the people who he and they hated. They, without doubt, were all good heterosexual family men. In fact, when I "traveled" that year I stayed at Frank's. One day, in the basement, Keith was there with his young son. When I came down the stairway, a funny thing happened. I told Frank in the 1990s that I was gay. He paused on the phone when I said it. And then he told everyone. A secret that I kept because of my shame was now a piece of candy to all the haters. When I said hello to Keith, he said nothing, and pulled his young son closer to him. I ignored it, and I got what I needed from the downstairs refrigerator, and I went back upstairs.

Pat told me that Frank paid more attention to Pliartrum than he did to his family. They took trips to the ocean in the summer every year when Boris was incarcerated on death-row. Now, they went to Pliartrum rallies. "You'll have a lot of fun," he told Sarah. Pat pulled Sarah closer to her. They went to three-rallies. "Two were there in the summer, and one, the most memorable, took place in forty-degree weather in the middle of a cornfield in 2020 in upstate New York," Frank, paid their twenty-dollar Pliartrum parking fee, which the candidate proclaimed was a donation to his campaign. Frank had already given Pliartrum money, and he was encouraged by his supervisors from the governor's office, to set up an automatic deduction once per month. That's when Lily looked a little closer at him. Pliartrum was a crook. All his pain centers and pain retreats were tax-havens for the so-called billionaire. Pliartrum took a cut of everything. When a company approached him for the rights to sell Pliartrum trading cards. He received a cool million, Lily thought, which, she said, "he also received a cool million from several people that he pardoned before he left office, and another million for him and Rich, Jr. — They offered color-commentary to a judo event in Hong Kong.

Hundreds of Pliartrum's people were brewing. They went through security, and, quickly, the area cordoned off with yellow tape filled up like a rock concert. Whenever I talked to Frank, I knew that I talked with Glenda and Uncle Stu at the same time. She added that they had to park a mile away from the rally site. "The wind was terrific," she said. Pliartrum arrived by helicopter, spoke his usual rant for an hour and forty-minutes, he got back in the helicopter and took off. There were no buses or shuttles to and from the rally site. "We were freezing as we walked the mile back to the pick-up truck, which was parked in a cornfield," she recollected. Sarah never endured the trip because she went to her friend's house that weekend; her "safe house. Before the 2020 Presidential Election, in 2018, Pliartrum lost his Country Club majorities in both the House of Representative and the Senate. Frank devoted all his free time to Pliartrum's campaign. Besides canvassing, he also became a troll. Pliartrum's people gave him names and email addresses, and he sent messages in the name of Pliartrum, to households all over the State. In them, he harassed voters for their devotion to the People Party, as well as their feelings toward the former leader. Frank never told me if he had ever made threats in his communiques. I would have said, no way, before Pliartrum. Now, I wouldn't put it past him.

I thought, once, if I could clap my hands or ring a bell, I would do so, to break the spell that Frank, Uncle Stu, and a lot of good Americans who were under the power of Glenda, with her PROX news mishegoss and Pliartrum. As the election drew closer, I used every argument I thought of. I sent an email to my brother: "Can you imagine your grandchildren's future, under Pliartrum, and his ilk, where it's organized crime who rules America." He would simply use another one of Glenda/Pliartrum's talking points. The dishonesty and thuggery of Pliartrum, and, in turn, the Country-Club Party members was so blatant, that I knew it was *Malefic*. The old country-club members, who still cared about this country, and who wanted to continue with our form of government. Pliartrum people were blinded by *M-workers*, who acted on orders. *Malefic* wanted to test each person's morality levels, just like it was done to the German people back in the 1930s, and probably throughout history.

Pliartrum's message spread throughout the land like a virus. To me it was as bad as the pandemic. A lot of innocent people could lose their lives, once again, thanks to Glenda, PROX News, and president dimwit.

The night of the Presidential Election, Glenda interviewed Pliartrum. He never touted that he simply would go away, lick his wounds, and live to fight another day. "But that's not Pliartrum," Lily told me. "He announced the night the election was stolen from him, even before the results were announced. He had done it before.

"When he ran in 2016, and 2020, he did the exact same thing," Lily told me. He announced on a talk show, a few months before the election, that if he didn't win then it was stolen from him. That's because, she said "he's the leader of organized crime in America. He's never going to abandon that. He was only a toy-soldier before he received the Country Club nomination in 2016. "When he won," Lily said, "He had real power for four-years, but he knew nothing about government or the Presidency. He only knew how to use "muscle." He was a dunce and a thug, and, thanks to *Malefic*, he got past the law, who should've been on his ass for all his crimes decades ago. But *Malefic* had other motives, I believed. For example: The feds were blinded; Pliartrum skirted the IRS by dumping hundreds of thousands of documents attached to income tax returns each year, too many for anyone to go through, so they always accepted his word."

"In his first term, he was a piece of driftwood in an ocean. He never learned how to ride the damn thing. The country gets by because of his ineptness. The guy was all brawn. He copied his heroes, the mafia thugs of yesteryear, who all ended up in prison, which was where I think he should've been long ago, along with every elected official who was in cahoots with him on *J6*," Lily wrote.

There were many, and each Country Club House Member and those in the Senate who held office, must face legal consequences for fraud against the American People, Lily felt. Not one should be allowed to serve in the United States government again. The other thug organizations: Pee-Boys, Nazis and a host of other scum, who lived under a rock, and, for the first time, they had a soapbox thanks to technology, and it was their man in power. Pliartrum's crookedness rivaled that of Tutin in Russia, who he bowed to and kissed his ring. Later, as all crooks eventually do, he messed up. He miscalculated and it opened the door for Pliartrum, not only to be, possibly, the President of the United States, and the leader of organized crime in America, he now saw himself, with Tutin in trouble, as the Leader of organized crime in the world. President Rich Pliartrum saw himself as the most powerful man in human history.

Pliartrum triggered a mass psychosis in America that never happened in the Country's history. The civil war was not triggered by a psychopath. This megalomaniac was an idiot that the World, yet alone the States, had not seen since the likes of Adolf Hitler. And the good common-sense people of America understood. But Lily believed that Pliartrum was the kind of person, when he tasted real power, it was, in his mind, forever. He looked upon himself as a historic figure who stood out. In his mind he was right up there with Genghis Khan, Alexander the Great and Napoleon. "He became, in his mind," Lily said: *"The Godfather* of organized crime in the country." Lily's YouTube video comment and his post that followed it, proved it. He had a serious mental illness on top of it all. Lily once told me that if he won the Oval Office, again, it would take a swat team to get him out of there.

When Frank was a boy scout. Mom thought he needed a father figure. She knew the scout leader, so she enrolled him. Frank earned many merit badges. What he picked up helped him and he grew. He discovered that he loved politics. One night he was introduced to the Country Club party, he was smitten with it. As a county tax-collector, he formed opinions about his fellow man. He used to be timid when we were young. His timidity shifted to cynicism and hostility towards others. Pliartrum's hate and cruelty was a drug to him, and he felt empowered by it.

The years went by. Pliartrum's election bid failed in 2020, but not in 2024. It wasn't the first time in World History that I thought about it. They perverted mankind. Their philosophy was extended to the masses. *Malefic* in consultation with the *Executives*, who sought guidance from *God*, which, with misfortune, a decision to see, ultimately, if *Malefic* was ordered to have the *M-team* construct a path to teach the ultimate lesson to mankind once again. *M-watchers* ordered *M-workers* to create a path for the madness of a people to carry out the unthinkable. Another path was for the poor souls that passed through the horror. It happened. The groups were there. The atmosphere caused the minds of the people to be triggered. It took one man, Adolf Hitler, to pull it. *Malefic*, through Hitler, tested modern mankind; it failed miserably.

Chapter 5

After Manuel broke Lily's arm and he was banned until he cleaned up his act. In the meantime, Lily had surveillance cameras installed. They were mounted in five-areas inside and outside of the home. Police found the areas where they were installed. They were ripped from their mountings. The whereabouts of the devices remained unknown. Lily's cell phone was also missing. Detective Jackson and his team scoured the home for a week. They found, absolutely, nothing in the way of physical evidence. Circumstantially there was evidence. Detective Jackson knew of Manuel's assault on Lily, and he obtained information from family members. Sam told him about Lily's and Manuel's history. He had compiled enough circumstantial evidence that Manuel was called in for his second interrogation. Detective Jackson wanted to break him.

The room had become all too familiar to Manuel. The youth took a seat and glanced up at the surveillance camera. He smiled for a split second. Jackson was joined by another detective, Lenny, who remained silent the entire time that Detective Jackson and Manuel dueled. It was "an Academy Award performance," the silent detective wrote in his notes, which Sam obtained long after the events. The detective asked: "Manuel tell me what happened from the beginning." The silent detective told Sam that they typically did that. They looked for inconsistencies. Manuel retold the story; he delivered his words with the expression, which indicated that he'd said the words before. "Like, I already told you, you're wasting my time," Lenny scribbled the words on his pad. There was one area of contention. Where were the surveillance devices and Lily's cell phone. After he finished his recital, Manuel scooted forward and leaned back in the chair. Jackson took the opportunity to cross examine him about the day's interrogation. He compared it to the first. This time he used Manuel's statement that he lived on the other side of the house and that he heard nothing around the time of death the coroner had determined. Manuel's physical communication showed that he was outraged. He scooted back in his seat and sat up. His facial expression indicated his astonishment as the silent detective recounted it.

"So, what are you trying to say, exactly? Manuel asked. "That I had something to do with the murder of my mother. That is an insult. How dare you accuse me. I loved my mother."

Jackson brought up Lily's broken arm. Manuel explained the typical pushing and shoving and claimed that "it doesn't mean that I murdered the person that I loved. I'd been with her since the age of four. I worshiped my mother. I am offended, frankly. I did not murder her. I loved her with all my heart."

The detectives looked at each other for a second: Detective Jackson looked back at Manuel and told him: "You're good. You are very good."

Manuel exploded; contrition was the last thing on his mind. "I'm good. I'm very good," "Oh, my God, I can't believe this. You think I'm acting?"

Jackson stated simply: 'No, I think you're a sociopath."

"A sociopath? You think that I am a sociopath! I swear. I'm so insulted right now. Don't you understand that I loved my mom with all my heart and soul."

Jackson looked at Lenny, who shrugged his shoulders. "Well," Jackson said, "let me tell you what I think really happened that night. You planned it all. You went into the garage and picked up the ax. You sharpened it on a stone just before you used it. You played what you wanted to do over and over in your mind. To you it solved your problem. You talked your way out of things before. You believe that you're good at that. She had crossed the line so many times, you rationalized. You must've moved down the hallway, just like Jack Nickolson in *The Shining*. You were determined to do what needed to be done with your sharpened tool. Your mother was asleep. Her light and television were on. With one swift blow you drove the ax into her skull. Her body convulsed," he said, "then she gurgled. You took all the CCT equipment, her purse and phone to the lake behind the house. You threw it in. Your phone, boy genius, was still in your back pocket. You retrieved it and called 911. Manuel shook his head, vehemently. "I did not murder my mother."

"Life with your mother was very cordial after you broke her arm. You stopped talking back. You were quieter, I learned from looking at her email to one of her friends. But with each constructive prompt, she gave you, you complied, but at the same time it ratcheted, what you cared for, up a notch. It must've brewed in you for a while. You had a plan. Like I said. You wanted to do what you did, but you did not want to face any consequences for it. In fact, during your first interrogation you wondered if this interfered with your future college plans. So, don't give me that shit that you didn't do it. Yes, you did! You were in her room! When you were banished from home, she installed an array of security equipment around the house. Cameras, motion detectors, the whole-nine-yards. You knew the equipment was there, Manuel. In fact, after you did it you dismantled all of it. You threw that and her purse into a lake behind the house. Days before you sneaked around. You spied on her that night when she was on the phone with her brother.

Manuel leaned forward and he pointed his finger at Detective Jacson, in a quivered voice he said, emphatically, "I did not murder my mother."

Later, outside the door, Jackson looked at his partner who shrugged his shoulders. "Okay," the detective came back, "I can see this is going nowhere." Jackson later told his peer: "Since there's no physical evidence, I can't draw a confession out of him. We have no other choice, but to drain the lake." Manuel was released again.

Chapter 6

Once a year, Sam visited Boris at the State Prison in Altoona, Pennsylvania. The incarcerated individual lost two appeals but he rallied support for clemency. The twenty-six-year-old had many close shaves but nothing panned out. His case was in the hands of the Supreme Court. The last time Sam saw his nephew was when he stepped into the "metal box," as he called it. Boris and Sam were separated by thick glass. The two men each picked up the phone receiver and the first word out of Boris' mouth that day was: Why? He never understood why he did what he did. He'd seen many counselors over his young life but nothing ever sunk in. Sam thought it was time that they had a heart-to-heart talk. Boris never knew that Sam was mentally ill and that for most of his life his Uncle Sam worked in that arena of the mind. Sam wrote to Boris and he told the young death row inmate that he was bipolar. The elder Isaac went on to tell the young man that he had APD and ASPD. When each were juvenile delinquents Boris never Sam wanted Boris to understand mental illness and criminality in order to draw a picture for the lad about Malefic. The incarcerated man learned about people's pathways in life and the choices a person had. Boris knew nothing about Sam because Frank, not being a storyteller, never talked to him about it. Also, because Boris spent more quality time with his Aunt Glenda as a little kid. But now he heard the truth about life from Sam, and just like the kids in the elementary school things sunk in.

Sam never knew that he had ASPD. "It's triggered through a person's genetics and environment," Sam told Boris. "But that never meant what you did was forgivable. You're still responsible. You were given the path to do the crime by Malefic because you fantasized; you saw yourself doing it and that you yearned for it in your heart. Sam explained, in depth, what he had learned over time. Sam told his relation, on the other side of the glass, that Malefic played with a person's mind. "You should've used your right and wrong skills; common sense is something we all come equipped with, " he told him. He added: "then you should've never walked on the darkened path that Malefic had tempted in the first place. It should've been rejected. But you didn't stop, you embraced it and you hopped aboard the Malefic express to Hell. "Boris, Sam counseled, you could have stopped at any time along the way that day. Malefic always gave a person time to stop and think when they arrived at the zone that most people never cross. You should've stopped before you acted out but, my God, you didn't. It's one thing to have the thought to murder someone. Most people reject those messages from hell out of hand as nonsense or gibberish because they would never do anything like that. In fact, they feel a little guilty for thinking that way. People fail, Boris, because life is all a big test. I know those feelings were a powerful urge. But you should've ignored the temptations because you knew, deep down, that it was wrong." Boris broke eye contact with Sam and he looked down. Sam thought, at that moment, that his nephew understood. Sam's enlightened family member was heavily medicated with psychotropic medications. A minute passed and Boris looked Sam in the eyes and said: "Thank you." Then Boris hung up and he gazed at Sam for a solid minute. Both sets of Isaac eyes locked on to each other. Malefic indicated in its report about Sam that at that moment the connection between the two was strong. Sam told him that each person had just as much right to live as the next person.

Boris had his supporters. He found religion over the last decade. He contacted two Rabbis who sent letters of support to the Governor. They asked for a reprieve based on Boris' age when the crime occurred. They pleaded to reduce his sentence to life without parole. They claimed that his remorse was genuine and that he recognized he was seriously mentally ill, but that he took responsibility for his actions. The Rabbis also sought support from one of the State's House of Representatives. Unfortunately, he was a member of the Country Club Party. The "I don't care" politician refused. But the People Party House Member invited him to his local office and his assistant listened, but her support could not stop Boris' final appeal. He had received a reprieve twice over the decade he sat on the death row. Through those years Boris had his ups and downs. The Rabbis provided the prayers for the dead. They acted to comfort the young man. Sam, however, never thought about what happened next. Before he rose, Boris told Sam that he had a girlfriend. He said that she wrote him a letter after he was sentenced, and, according to him, they hit it off. They write letters to each other each week. She lived in Ohio, and worked as a lab technician at one of Pliartrum's pain centers.

Chapter 7

The thrill ride that Sam "traveled" had so many inclines, dips and curves that he learned but he was still blinded, and he had no insight. He never readied himself for anything; how could he? There were so many things to prepare, and he never knew what was going on. He possessed knowledge and significant lessons. He understood, later, that he absorbed them consciously and subconsciously. Some were simple which he acted upon. Sam Martin Isaac was blinded by Malefic. He was never ready. He wallowed in his troubles. M-workers bit him with mind crippling cluster headaches and he despaired because insight was impossible.

When Bill escorted Sam out of the building, he felt no shame. He was not embarrassed. He didn't mind it at all. It never fazed him but it wasn't until later that he learned the reason why. It was all Malefic, and the M-team. He was rescued so many times but he never wondered or questioned anything. He never asked himself why because he was on track but he gained no insight; he wasn't supposed to. The mindless criminal never questioned the speed at which he was removed from trouble. He was aware of it, but never asked himself: Why was he always safe from the consequences? According to Malefic's report the subject never felt lucky, in a traditional sense because he was groomed to become a loser when it came to money. When he looked back on it, later in his life, when he reached adulthood, the memories of the supernatural interventions amazed him. He never gave thought to the fact that what happened should have amazed him. It didn't because he never thought about it. He never reflected on anything about his life in those years. He was relieved each time, hence, he never sought insight because he wasn't sitting in a prison cell; he was free to continue. He never figured out what it was all about. He only did that when there was a problem he encountered. When something went wrong and he wanted answers to resolve it so the trouble went away. That was his only focus. His cognition presented a plan to avoid trouble. Only then he asked. Otherwise, his blindness to his world continued unabated.

Those years that should've amazed him even more but they never did because he was down and the referee stood over him with the countdown to his demise. So, when it came to Malefic's miracles he had no insight, yet alone knowledge, into its magical world. It wasn't until he sat at Lily's computer did it all hit home. At this point he was too busy dealing with his mental health jobs, cluster headaches, and his own mental health history which changed drastically, once he gained the knowledge and plugged it into his life experiences. As far as he knew he was just depressed, thus he took antidepressants. The medication masked the truth from him until he realized that his mental health went far beyond the notion that it was just depression. The unbelievable incidents rested in his subconscious mind for him to tap into later. He acknowledged what occurred but the reasoning as to why escaped him. The answers and resolutions were buried deep in his mind in an area where it rooted. Subconsciously, his mind gave it sanctuary until the right moment that Malefic and the M-team carefully planned for; it was a haven until Sam was ready. His deep reflection into himself and the strange world he found himself in didn't blossom until everything in his life was in the right place. It took decades and his mental health jobs, along with his own psychological experiences until they were processed into his conscious being.

But his depression always led him back to the VA, and since he had no income he received free medical care. He saw a psychologist once a month. He was on psychotropics, which were prescribed by his psychiatrist, Doctor Wesson, who he saw every six-months. For three years, he paddled water. His Social Security Disability application was denied twice. The third time, it required that he appeared before a Social Security Judge but, in the meantime, something happened that changed his future.

He was surprised. However, at the same time it was right in front of his nose for thirty-years. Once again, he failed. He made no progress. He still wasn't ready. He remained blind. No access was granted; these mysteries all just piled up inside of him. Soon, it happened. Insight was generated. He thought, facetiously, that it was all piled up as crap in his mind, and it was brought on by all the pressure in his brain from the cluster headaches. Suddenly, the insight slowly dripped into him; its wisdom was absorbed by his coffer. A lot of his questions were answered but not all. He heard the diagnostic terms before so a lot of it, quickly, fit into place.

One day, he was at the VA. His monthly appointments continued for three-years with his psychologist, Doctor Miller but in sessions with him and every mental health professional he spun his wheels the entire time. He held onto his history of criminality. He never disclosed it to Doctor Miller or anyone, ever. When Sam finished his monthly appointment with him Doctor Wesson caught him as he left the psychologist's office. "I want to set a diagnostic appointment with you. He heard the term before. He knew it was the longest appointment that one could have with a psychiatrist; it went on for two-hours. Every answer that he provided she entered her computer. Her questions focused on his history. He only told her how he picked up and "traveled," but he omitted his crazy teenage escapades. He remembered clearly that she dazed-out for a second when he spoke of the times that he"traveled." She froze and softly uttered: "*guilty*." Sam saw that what he said clicked in her mind when she said that word to herself. As he watched her, for that nick of time, when she reacted, queerly, to her own observation. She asked: "Have you ever had a period in your life where you felt extremely good, and you slept very little, but you had a lot of energy?

Sam told her what he experienced. He recalled the wonderment of it all. "I felt so fantastic," he told her, "It lasted for weeks," he said. She stopped typing, looked up at her patient and said: "You're bipolar." He knew dozens of people with that diagnosis. He knew that it was a mood disorder, but he never knew any specifics. When, finally, he learned of the behaviors that led to a diagnosis; it hit him like an anvil. How stupid could he be to miss something as important as that. Or was it that he, simply, was blinded for all those years for a reason. The diagnosis was right in front of him the whole time. There was no other explanation. Malefic never wanted him to know because once diagnosed he studied any information he saw and he plugged into his own life; it all came together in his mind.

Once he knew about his bipolar, he processed a lot of his past. Some things started to make sense to him. He acknowledged the reality as he gained insight and he scribbled notes on scratch paper as to why he was the way he was. Ever since he was accepted into the VA it encouraged him to understand his mental health past and to do something; he became a mental health detective of sorts. He went to counseling, groups and medication. But he never talked about his criminality. Nothing was out of bounds. So, he sought financial relief from the VA because of the sexual assaults fifty years ago. He was diagnosed with PTSD, and he sought service-connected disability compensation. In his claim, he explained what happened a half-century ago, and how it had impacted his adult life. He wrote about his social isolation. He relayed information about his lack of friends. He admitted that he never sought romance. He spoke of the nightmares and flashbacks but what also ate at him was the family aspect of it all. Those wounds were raw and exposed and it stayed that way for another decade.

In the meantime, he had applied for Social Security Disability. He got notice of a date for a hearing before a judge. Immediately, he reached out because when a person went before a Social Security Judge, they needed representation. He knew it from experience. As a psychiatric case manager he had accompanied clients to their own Social Security hearings and each had representation.

Johnson, Brick and Meaker, Attorneys-at-Law, was the number one, Social Security disability, law office in town. Sam understood what took place and he shuddered at the thought of one. As a client now he never wanted an attorney because they took a big chunk if he won his case. But reality set in, and he called them. Kathy Swabb was an attorney-assistant. She had a secretary, which was who Sam spoke with initially. The actual lawyers of the firm had no involvement with any of it. The secretary wanted to know specific information: One, the nature of the potential client's disability, particularly his social media account information. Sam told her that he had more than one disability. He was diagnosed with PTSD, bipolar and cluster headaches. He also told her that he had a noncancerous brain tumor, according to an MRI. He told her that he's never been on social media. The lawyer representative told him that they would get back to him. So, he awaited a decision as to representation. The secretary called Sam the next day. She told him that his case was accepted. His hearing was six-months away. He was able to get by, only, because of Ellen. When he arrived in Las Vegas after he "traveled" again, he paid her for more than a year until his money ran out. He sought and received food stamps, and Ellen patiently waited three years for his Social Security Disability decision.

Those times weren't easy according to Malefic's summary, however. He read about President Pliartrum's crackdown on all kinds of social safety nets which benefitted poor people who utilize the resources of the Federal Government. People on Social Security Disability became an obsession with the command and chief. Some judges had their hands tied. They were forced to deny based on stricter criteria. Others, reportedly, reveled in their cruelty to dismiss what an applicant claimed. The process itself was very dysfunctional.

The big event was months away. Finally the law firm representative called Sam and set up an appointment for him to meet his rep, Sandy. When he met with her, they discussed the hearing and his case. In ten-days, he appeared before the judge. His pre-court meeting with Sandy didn't go well. He felt uncomfortable and defensive as she asked him questions. She pushed his buttons that day, and he left with a soggy feeling as if he urinated in his pants. Three days and a week passed and he entered the Federal Building, and he cleared security. He entered the outer office of the courtroom and he took a seat. When Kathy arrived, she said something about the judge because since Pliartrum entered the Oval Office her success in the court was.nill. Sam side-stepped what she said and he told her: "You pushed my buttons the other day." She looked at her client and said: "I was only asking you questions that the judge will ask." Sam replied in earnest: "Well, that's not going to happen today." For the first time in his messed up life he was super serious. He felt no nerves. He never feared the judge like he was the Cowardly Lion and that he stood before *The Wizard of Oz.*

His name was called. When he went through the door into the courtroom, immediately, his eyes met the Judge's eyes who was raised above him. The client and his representative were, at least, 10 yards away but when their eyes linked, the overseer of Social Security Disability, Judge Willam C. Taylor was taken aback. Sandy sat at one table. Sam was at another. After he sat down, his dead serious feelings and expressions sat with him. The citizen looked up at the Judge again and once again the man who enforced laws was taken aback. Sam registered each non-verbal communication moment into his central nervous system. First, Judge Taylor questioned Sam about a medical condition he had but never included in his claim: Sam's thyroid treatment. Taylor told the civilian: "The first disability you claim is your thyroid."

Sam was shocked: "I never put that down as one of my disabling conditions! It's true, I do not have a thyroid anymore, it was radiated, and I take a little pill in the morning, which gives me my thyroid hormone. That's it. It is not a disability." Sam told him. Judge Taylor moved on and the hearing continued. The judge asked questions that Sam gave precise answers to. One asked of him was:

"Do you care for a pet?" the Judge inquired.

"No," Sam replied.

"How did you get to the hearing today?" he wondered.

"By car, I was dropped off," Sam told him.

Next he asked the seeker of disability benefits: "How many cluster headaches did you have last month."

Sam never hesitated and said: "Three." At that moment he wished he could have told him how many hit him before he had a steady supply of cannabis. Then he would have answered: "More than thirty!" But, of course, he never talked about it because it was illegal to use cannabis back then even for medical purposes. The hearing went on for twenty-minutes. Malefic decided to make an appearance on Sam's behalf. The supernatural system took control of him. Suddenly, out of nowhere Sam's right arm slowly reached out and up to his eye level. Sam's hand clenched. The applicant looked at his fist a foot away from his face and through his lips. Malefic bellowed four-words: *"I WILL NOT SUICIDE."* Sam's arm lowered and he never flinched. He knew that he never raised his arm. He never clenched his fist and those words were not his. They came through his being, but he never thought about it or initiated it. Without doubt it was Malefic, and the reason that he, later, was so sure about that was because it was so obvious to Sam what happened after he put two-and-two together as he sat at his late sister's laptop. Sam began to invest in himself. That's when he began his new era. He thought a lot about all those crazy years. He added everything up. His accounting was ongoing. He desperately wanted to solve the puzzle inside of him; it started from when he was a child. Gradually he understood and he was given full access to his subconscious mind where all of his nefarious action was stored for many decades. What Sam found was that Malefic had dealt with him ever since he was a child; he was mischievous even back then. Later, he understood that Malefic dealt with everybody, not just him.

At the conclusion of the hearing the judge looked at Sam and said: "I think I can make a decision on your case." The claimant rose; his poker demeanor continued even after he left Judge Taylor's courtroom. He met Sandy at the door. She said: "He can't deny this one." Out in the waiting area, Sandy told him that he did good, and then she escorted him to her office and gave him a bottle of water; he gulped the liquid down. Ellen picked him up that day. Three-weeks later, the Judge's decision came down. In the era of "disability scams," as Pliartrum and his people put it. The honorable servant of the Courts ruled in Sam's favor; he was given three-year's worth of benefits. He paid Ellen off, and after that he gave her three-hundred dollars a month for rent. In the meantime, M-planners, M-developers, and M-coordinators went over all the data and determined the facts. The M-team made recommendations to Malefic as to Sam's disposition and future. .

Sam still lived with Ellen, but he still "traveled." He looked on craigslist for housing along the Washington coast, and then he came across an ideal housing opportunity. A veteran, John, who was gay, lived alone on a private island off the Washington coast. He posted an ad, which Sam came across as he searched. The veteran offered to rent a room in his home. The rent was affordable, and he could meet it with his monthly check from Social Security. Sam emailed John and inquired about it. The potential landlord wrote back that he had another tenant but he planned to move out next month.

Years later, Sam realized how Malefic had shifted his tectonic plates which made up his brain. He never drove across the country again. For four-decades he had been on the road in between MH assignments from Malefic. The word came down. M-workers were ordered by the M-watchers to stand by because things were about to drastically change in Sam's life. The M-team reported to Malefic that Sam was finished with his mental health education and that it was time for him to address all of his other sore spots.

When Sam "traveled," he went, practically, everywhere in the continental US, except for States like Oregon and Washington because they were too far north. This time, however, that's where he planned to go. He still wanted a typical life. He never understood why he never had normal human experiences; he just had a lot of sex. There was never any love. Oh, he fretted about the lack of friendship and love in his life to psychologists and himself. But then he turned on the television and he accepted the solitude. He was, really, fine being alone. Some folks hated solitude he said to himself. Sam wished that he was one of them. He wanted a normal life. He believed he should've made friends; he should've had good relations with his family but that included relationships with others; he was simply transactional in his interactions with people. Sam learned that the reason why he never experienced basic human happenings was because his subconscious mind never budged; it held all of the secrets and he remained clouded to them until a new era of his life began on planet earth. Decades ago when Sam worked with SED children which was before he "traveled" and the cluster headaches started; he was diagnosed with APD. But there was another undiagnosed mental illness condition he should've been diagnosed with but wasn't because Sam refused to tell another soul about his teenage behaviors; he still carried those secrets with him which resulted in his lack of real insight.

A month went by and John, the guy on the island in Washington, wrote Sam an email. The prospective owner told him that the room was vacant. John also said that he needed somebody to take him into Seattle, for shoulder replacement surgery. He was inpatient for two-days. Sam quickly loaded his; he had it down to a science. Once there Sam took care of his dog. Once discharged from the hospital Sam picked up the proprietor; it was a two-hour drive, both ways.

Sam never figured this guy out until he arrived in Washington. The new tenant had no vehicle, but he needed to take a supply of cannabis with him, as well as his dog, Pearl. So, he deemed it impossible to fly there. He rented a car in Las Vegas. He rented a car and drove to the location sixty-miles west of Tacoma; it was about one-thousand miles from the gambling capital of the world. Once there Sam and his pooch took a ferry, which made trips between the island, where John lived, and the mainland.

Sam wallowed in his inability to have relationships. Men and women have laid beside him but he had no normal relationships. So, he never came close to one person who said he or she loved him. He was at the point in his life when he doubted that his mother and father ever said it. But more importantly, he recognized that he never said to another. He loved no one and no one loved him. It bothered him for decades; he tried to be social but he was never up to the task. However, this time he felt he could change. However, in spite of his bipolar, APD, and ASPD he felt determined to make his new home different. John had a very nice, two-story home which sat amongst other homes on the island; its circumference was a mile.

John had one thing on his mind the minute Sam arrived. He took his new tenant by the arm to his bedroom. Sam being sexualized during childhood by Tony, and his behaviors following the sexual assaults in the navy, meant he went to bed with anyone, regardless of race, nationality or gender. This time it was different, however nothing ever happened because it wasn't supposed to. There was no sexual urge or desire for sexual relations in Sam, Malefic sure of that and when the owner of the home tried to make a pass at him it didn't work and Sam told him took off his clothes but he was never aroused. Consequently, he never got it up. The change in him was for a reason; M-workers swarmed around him and made certain that nothing happened because he never felt a rise in his crouch, not to mention the yearning in his mind. He drove John into Seattle to the VA Medical Center the next day for his surgery and he went back to the island and cared for John's dog and Pearl.

After the Social Security decision, Sam wanted a dog just like Rusty. Pearl came to him through the internet. She was the most beautiful mutt that he ever saw. The M-team, again, engaged in the unbelievable. He wanted a dog and Malefic determined that Sam needed a dog. A woman posted the ad just twenty-minutes before he found it online.

The pooch made a difference in his life. Like a man and a woman, a woman and a woman or a man and a man, people's life circumstances and Malefic brought the two together. Immediately, he called about the dog. She gave away a two-year-old canine who was mixed between a chihuahua and a dachshund. The new owner named her Pearl. She was sweet just like Rusty. She had caused problems in the young women's home, however. Sam saw that Pearl was loved immensely by her. But she had a boyfriend who was six-four and weighed three-hundred pounds. When she arrived at the location to meet Sam watched as she held his new pet. The woman's face looked pained. She looked like she had cried. Her boyfriend, however, looked angry. She asked Sam if he would give her beloved dog a lot of petting. Sam told her that he would. She handed her to him. It was a wonderful moment for the mentally ill man, something he rarely felt. Sam's M-workers, unbeknownst to him, cheered the new arrival. As the broken hearted lady left her M-workers consoled her sadness. The reason that she gave the dog away was because Sam learned that Pearl was not housetrained nor was she familiar with a leash.. She had never been taken on a walk. Then he put two and two together. The huge boyfriend must have stepped into Pearl's poop for the last time. It most likely happened before and she was warned the next time it happened the canine was out. Sam concluded that it was the next time. The new owner walked her twice a day and he successfully housetrained her. The sixteen-pound animal accompanied him as he drove north to an area of the country that he had never seen. Sam convinced himself when he traveled this time it was not like when he "traveled" before because this time he knew where he was going.

Sam liked his room at John's. The habitable room was on the second floor. The owner's bedroom was on the first floor. Sam moved all his possessions which included, by this time, his supply of medical marijuana was as a secret to John.

They got along before John went into the hospital. They arrived at the dock and took the ferry across the island. He drove John's car because his rental car remained on the isle. The M-team thwarted any sexual antics. Retrospectively, Sam was glad. He was less interested in it, for some reason. After he picked John up at the hospital things changed. Sam never paid John any rent. The way the former Las Vegas resident had figured it; he drove up, at his own expense but it was at his request to help him when he went in for surgery. The whole thing was crazy, but Sam never realized it as it happened. He took care of the guy's dog and his home while John was in the hospital. Sam assisted him as a caregiver for two-days. He bathed him and dried him. He even clipped his disgusting toenails. As they ate dinner the landlord asked his new tenant for money. Sam put down his fork and said: "What?"

Later, it registered in Sam's mind that John screwed him because he learned about John's hobby. He had other people who emailed him about the Island. Sam heard him, downstairs, on his computer. The man drank from a bottle of wine, as he hooted and hollered at pornographic images online. That information exposed to Sam that he wasn't the first person he did this to because he sent images of himself as a prerequisite to living there.

Sam realized, later, it was all a part of his ongoing project with Malefic and Sam's M -team because a major incident happened on the island the next day. John agreed to look at something that Sam wrote. The writer brought his laptop into John's bedroom. Suddenly, Sam tripped. The laptop flew out of his hands and crashed into one of John's large "expensive" vases on the floor; it broke apart and laid in ruin. John never asked Sam if he was okay. The man with the new shoulder just flipped out and started screaming at his lessee.

"Look what you did! Look at what you fucking did! Either you pay me $600, or I want you out of my house! I don't want to look at your goddamn laptop or anything you wrote! I want you out!"

Sam's hand went through the little bit of hair that he had. Sam stormed upstairs in distress. He had to get out of there, but where to? It was so sudden and Sam became distressed. He looked at Pearl and cried.

He couldn't afford a room at an establishment but he needed out, even if it meant that he was homeless. John knew the VA system. He told Sam he knew someone who obtained housing through the VA in Tacoma. Pearl and Sam were on their own as they sat in the rental car as they crossed the icy waters. The now homeless man and his dog were homeless. He had loaded some of his possessions into the vehicle even though most of his possessions remained on the island. John allowed him to put most of it into his garage and later he could come for it once he settled in somewhere. Sam and Pearl drove around Tacoma for two-days in the rental car because he couldn't find the homeless shelter. He stopped many times and asked for directions but he just could never find it. As it turned out, all that time, he looked for the wrong street. There were two Harvest Streets, one north of downtown and one south of it. For two nights they slept in the cold car at the parking lot of a McDonald's.

Later, Sam credited Malefic for the run-around. Sam handled his predicament. He and Pearl toured around Tacoma and he carried with him some frustration. He fretted over his internet connection with John and all the money he wasted on his trip north.

Sam questioned, in particular, the timing when he tripped, and destroyed John's "expensive" vase. He never imagined the unbelievable series of events which followed. When they finally arrived at the shelter, on his third day, a homeless shelter staff member who processed Sam's application petted Pearl, who stood by very patiently. Sam was lucky the shelter allowed dogs. Suddenly, the staffer looked at Sam and stated: "You don't have any drugs. I don't have to search your bags." Once again, M-workers intervened because, of course, he had an ounce of marijuana in one of his bags. Malefic blinded Sam; he had no desire to use the substance while he was at the shelter either overtly or covertly. The M-team blocked his impulses and he never had the urge to use it. Later, when tempted, however, he failed because one day, during his six-week stay, he searched his bags. He never saw it. He had no cluster headaches while he and Pearl stayed there. But, for some reason, he wanted to make sure he still had it. He scoured his bags and he never located it. But it was there the whole time because weeks later, when he was about to leave, he found it. The stuff was there the whole time; it made Sam scratch his head. He never processed anything about his life because it was just like all of his other escapades; the answers lay dormant inside his subconscious mind until the time was right.

Soon, Sam arrived at the shelter and he took public transportation to the VA Medical Campus. Cindy Kazel worked at the VA for ten-years. She helped homeless veterans. Sam was homeless and as he sat and listened to her he scratched his head.

And then it all happened. It was Malefic. There was no doubt, he said to myself years later. He walked closer to the solution of his angst over all these years that day; she blew up the log jam in Sam's mind. Cindy asked him a question."How would you describe your quality of life?" Immediately, the veteran teared up. The question must have pushed his buttons because, uncharacteristically, he shot back:

"Are you kidding me?"

Sam talked about his life outside of his work when he was employed in the MH field. He told her that he had a very empty life. Then she asked him if he had a service-connected disability and if he ever applied for one. He told her about the two sexual assaults and how they impacted his life.

At this point Sam had never processed what happened with Tony when he was a child; he hadn't an ounce of insight.

"No family, friends or romance?" she asked.

"My family doesn't care about me. I am friendly to all people, but I have no friends. As for romance, I never had a relationship."

"Have you applied for a service-connected disability?" she inquired.

"I applied twice, and they were both denied," he answered.

"Well, you need to see a VA compensation specialist," she advised.

I said: "It'll just be denied again because there's no proof except for the history of my life.

Sam told her about John and how he "traveled" from Las Vegas.

"Is that where you applied for your service-connected disability claim?" she wondered.

"Yes," he replied.

"Well, we do things a little differently around here," she said.

Sam recognized when he thought about it, years later, that his demeanor in MH, which he used for thirty-years, kicked in, automatically, while he resided at the shelter. The mood, the confidence, and the kindness drove him just like it did before. Although, he helped another homeless veteran in a case manager type situation while he was at the shelter. He and Pearl got along with everyone they encountered at the shelter and that's when Sam realized what an icebreaker she was.

After he arrived at the single-story building. He looked around the open court that led into the haven. It was filled with many men who waited in the cold to go inside. People's frigid breaths met up with the cigarette smoke that arose in their midst. Sam looked at the faces of the unfortunate as he sat on a bench next to one of his peers. Mike was from Tacoma. His wife threw him out when he returned home drunk last night. He spoke up first and asked Sam what his dog's name was. "Pearl," he said: "She's beautiful," he said as he petted the mutt. Poverty and despair were evident in the buzz of men's murmured voices; it all looked and sounded very dark.

The VA compensation specialist met Sam that night. She completed her paperwork, and she told him that he'd get a letter from the VA soon. Next in the process he was to meet with a psychologist, for their assessment.

Once at the homeless shelter it never entered his mind to go back to Las Vegas. So, he waited in limbo for housing. Shelter staff gave Sam a mat and a blanket. Pearl slept by his feet as they lay on the tiled floor with fifty other men. To Sam, as he looked back, the magic was too unbelievable because remarkable things happened. What amazed Sam the most was the way everything was timed and fell into place. Malefic wanted Sam to jump through many hoops; he decided later when he reached that period during his insight. He never dreamt that his trip north led to financial security. But it did, and it changed his life. He never questioned anything that happened at that time. Just like in his early years, he was not in control of events.

He turned in the mat and blanket when he was told that he could move into the veteran's room. There were nine actual beds and nine vets. Even though dogs were allowed at the homeless shelter there were no other dogs present during Sam's stay. The guys loved Pearl. Occasionally, Sam saw that she slept in other veterans beds.

Five weeks passed and one night Sam collapsed at the shelter. An ambulance was called and he was rushed to a local hospital. Within an hour the hospital staff released him. It was one o'clock in the morning as he walked back to the shelter. During his walk back he collapsed again, this time on a residential sidewalk. He tried but he couldn't stand because each time he attempted it he fell back to the ground. He laid there for hours. Suddenly, he opened his eyes and he saw a woman who stood over him with a walkie-talkie in her hand. He told her: "I fell and I couldn't get up." An ambulance arrived and it took him back to the hospital that he came to from the shelter. He had just spent the night where he lied on the sidewalk of a city that had a high crime rate. Later, with all of his insight, Sam realized that he was protected by Malefic that night.

Sam was in the hospital for a week; he had pneumonia. After he was discharged, he went back to the shelter. The social worker at the hospital arranged for him and Pearl to fly back to Las Vegas.

His trip north helped himself tremendously but he never realized it. When he lived at the Red Cross shelter Sam helped another homeless veteran with his case management needs. The man that Sam helped served during Vietnam and he received six-hundred dollars per month from Social Security Disability. Sam knew there was a program for veterans like him. It guaranteed, a former service member, one-thousand dollars per month. He introduced him to the VA uncompensated Specialist who helped him, and she was on it right away. The money owed to the uncompensated man was an amount that changed a life. He was due about thirty-thousand dollars, when backdated.

Chapter 8

Sarah spent a lot of time at the Sherman residence. Her friend, Cathy, was a wonderful pianist according to Sarah. Her friend lived in a large brick home, not far from where Sarah grew up. It was in a nice section of the town. Her dad was a doctor, and her mom a volunteer worker at a nursing home. The girls met at the sorority they both belonged to. Their shared interest included Cathy's talent on the piano not to mention basketball. Cathy loved to compose music to words and Sarah wrote poems. They worked together; "just like Lennon and McCartney," Doctor Sherman once said.

Well before Sarah walked to Cathy's house, when the weather was bitterly cold, in the wee hours of the morning, Frank boarded a chartered-bus and headed for Washington, D.C. There were twelve-buses loaded with individuals who espoused Pliartrumism. They were all headed for the Nation's capital; it was January 6, 2021. Frank, who never entered the Capital that day, stood in the cold to support Pliartrum, who was still in his first term as President. It was noon and Pliartrum took the podium behind thick bullet-proof glass. Frank stood amongst thousands of people who answered the President's call to come to the Nation's Capital city on that momentous day. "Be there it will be wild," The Commander in Chief posted to his followers on social media.

Malefic's power was on display that day. M-workers twisted the minds of the faithful, and they were blinded and fed a steady diet of propaganda and misinformation. Glenda was the queen of J6, if you asked Sam. She outright lied to her viewers every night.

The mass of hate congregated on the Ellipse that day. Frank went through security; he had no weapons but there were many in the raucous crowd. Those who supported Pliartrum were fine with America being ruled by the thugs of organized crime. The only force that could create such an historic event and to carry it out on this scale was Malefic. The last time the supernatural force tested a nation was in Germany, in the 1930s, when it was under Hitler and Nazi rule. The pathway was open and millions of Germans walked upon it. Lily warned Sam that Americans would be susceptible to it as well.

The roar of the crowd who gathered in mass sounded like a pack of hungry wolves according to one participant. The Stars and Stripes flag was smeared that day and the greatest catastrophe for the country since the American civil war. That day Frank and his buddies whooped and hollered when the President spoke. Frank did not participate in what happened next. Instead, he was sidelined with his phone against his ear as he stuck a finger, from his other hand, into his other ear; he wore the I can't hear you expression. Malefic and the countless M-teams and more than a trillion M-workers worked overtime that day.

Book 3

Chapter 1

On the 6th of January 2021, President Pliartrum did what he did best; he manipulated thousands of people to do his bidding by lying to them and it split the county's population by using an old strategy of his; he overwhelmed his enemies with a deluge of force, fibs and deceit. Before he became Commander in Chief, every year, for decades, his business strategy flooded the Internal Revenue Service with millions of tax documents. He inundated them with their own product. Consequently, he set into motion perpetual audits that kept him and his businesses virtually tax free because of the auditors inability to make sense of it all. The tactics he used dammed up the gears of the federal government, in particular, the IRS. But Pliartrum had more than the taxman that he hated and wanted to punish his enemies, particularly in the federal government; it was his alphabet soup: The FBI, ATF, DOD, ICE, all under DOJ and DHS and practically stemmed from his deeply He accomplished his goal and cheated the feds on his personal and business tax obligations. He created thousands of LLCs (Limited Liability Companies) and they were key to his tax scheme; he exploited them mercilessly. Every year his taxes overwhelmed the institution which made it impossible to reign in the tax cheat. On J6, however, the battle was not over taxation; it was because of power and greed; he ripped the fabric of the entire nation for his own personal gain.

Pliartrum and his organized crime gang overwhelmed and slashed the nation's lifespan of stability which followed the civil war. These criminals intimidated people with tactics straight out of *The Godfather* and it created a huge crisis for the country. He superseded the 19th Century's bitter civil war with an undeclared conflict between good and evil. Honest folks and thuggish criminals. He birthed a bloodless civil war between his followers and institutions like the civil service which relied heavily on employing based on merit rather than political hacks. No one was safe in government. He picked fights with the media and institutions of commerce and of learning which consisted of individuals who were diametrically opposed to him and his inept control over the truth, justice, and freedom. The American way went the wrong way. Pliartrum stoked the division between the masses when it came to morality. The president's morality had already been determined to be a fat zero. He was the president from hell and he was hell bent on his declaration; he wanted complete control of the Federal government that included the judiciary, members of the House of Representatives, and the Senate. His lackeys filled the government positions. Pliartrum never governed; he only ruled. All of his time was spent fighting the rule of law and when he wasn't doing that he was golfing. Pliartrum became the leader of organized crime in America when he crossed the threshold of the Oval Office. Before that he was just a player in the ranks of the country's criminal element. His criminality knew no bounds. He fought everyday not for the American people but for himself; he strategized against the country's laws; he never swayed from his goal. He dominated his perceived enemies like a sadist who was filled with cruelty and evil. He watched as they suffered from his edicts; it was all entertainment to him. He reveled in it. He sank to unimaginable and ridiculous depths when he was unable to control his impulsivity and he addressed Lily's comment online. According to

Malefic's report she was an average citizen who wrote a critical comment about the former and now current President of the United States in response to a Youtube video. Sam was listed as a sibling which included photos of him at an anti-Pliartrum meeting. Another showed him at a rally where he marched with about 400 people. Also, the report indicated that he was placed on Pliartrum's enemies list because of his affiliations and activities. One was writing post cards from a voter registration list which he handwrote and mailed at his expense. He remembered Lily's words when his pen came to paper:

Dear Voter,

I'm writing to tell you that organized crime has taken over America. "Don't let organized crime rule America. Stop them before it's too late. Call your Senator at 212-445-3464. Thanks, Sam."

Psychopaths and sociopaths had control of the event on that brisk day. There were throngs of thugs and everyday people in attendance. As the event unfolded sinister forces meddled with their minds in the form of speeches which aroused the crowd into a lather in anticipation of the president's appearance and his speech. Pliartrum's team included a smorgasbord of hate groups that formed a coalition of evil with organized crime at the helm. The roots were the remnants of the nation's bitter war over slavery. The Old South confederacy had arisen from the ashes of history. The South lost the civil war, but now emerged from the grip of defeat, over 150 years ago, to where they were finally going to prevail. The coalition of hate included active members of hate mongers like the Pride Boys, Oats People, Klu Klux Klan, Neo-Nazis, White Supremacists, Christian Nationalist and consolers and controllers of the cause like PROX NEWS and other right-wing cable news networks who filled their viewers with pork; it was 24-hours of oinking and anger and hate-filled television everyday; they brainwashed good people exercising their hatred inside dormant in every soul. These groups along with their genuine fake news networks were dedicated to Pliartrum's movement. They out hustled everyday hustlers of the country club party into oblivion and there was not a good person, in their ranks, left standing.

"They sold their souls to the devil," was the way Lily described it before her demise.

These groups led Pliartrum's parade of gangsters, misfits, clowns, buffoons, idiots, and liars. Not to forget the pedofiles, like Pliartrum himself, who had a close association with the most evil sex-trafficer of children in modern history. They were best buddies and shared their methods of criminality. The two had a lot incommon:"These guys were like a wrecking crew." Besides pedofilia Pliartrum dabbled in money laundering and cocaine smuggling. The former, now current, president was also a front for the mob when casinos arrived on the Atlantic City boardwalk. These degenerate citizens skimmed millions of dollars until Pliartrum's casino doors closed and filed for bankruptcy.

Pliartrum's supporters loved him, no matter what he did. They gave him a free pass to trample on people's individual rights. He cared nothing about the Constitution; he never even read it. In fact, in his second term in office freedom and the "American way," were tested time and again. But Superman he was not. According to his wife's account in the billion dollar book deal she wrote. "My husband loves Hitler. The only things he read was either Mein Kampf or one of the Nazi leader's speeches. Pliatrum admired Hitler's long speeches which lasted, sometimes, for hours but he could only muster up an hour, or two, when he gave a speech: "Due to all of the moosh inside his brain," she wrote.

The consequential day was carefully planned and thought out. Along with Pliartrum's henchmen, whose psychosis spread through the mass of 50,000 people like a wildfire or a flash flood. The worst of them wreaked havoc on law enforcement officers and the US Capitol.

More people attended Pliartrum's first inauguration, however, that event garnered approximately 300,000 which was far less than his predecessor during his first term. But Pliartrum knew on that cold January day that the people in front of him were suckers and losers because they were his diehard sycophants.

Pliartrum's clan of evil congregated at his beckon call. Hundreds knew, in advance, that violence would take place. Frank was not one of them.

"I'm just going to hear Pliartrum's speech and show my support," Frank said to Pat the night before.

He rejected her warning not to go. On that day Frank and hundreds of others from Central Pennsylvania, had a short ride to the nation's capital; however, tens of thousands of Pliartrum's supporters traveled hundreds if not thousands of miles to be there. Most in the crowd had no idea what Pliartrum and his team had planned.

The stage was set and speaker after speaker hurled treasonous barbs at them, and the crowd ate it up like a hungry dog. As Frank stood in line to go through security he saw hundreds of "good people," according to him, who mingled outside the safety barrier. Each was armed with, at least, one weapon.

Chapter 2

Detective Jackson had a theory. He believed that a person who broke the law, murdered another and was conscious free, lived a precarious life void of guilt. He feared nothing, ergo his mind was void of guilt. The seasoned detective recalled from his studies in criminal justice 101. The SMI man never looked over his shoulders to see if he was being followed. The guilty individual never believed that he could be in any trouble. His whole being rejected any sense of emotion or even awareness about the consequences. There was no pride in what he did. There were no celebrations over it. It happened just as if he got in and out of his clothes every day. He never thought about it. He just did it. When he went into the navy he had no fear that he faced any trouble from his past. The criminal mind is very good at burying its misdeeds. In his mind it was as if crimes never occurred. Nothing happened in his mind after it. It was over. He moved on.

That's a class of sociopathy that Samual Isaac had no experience in. He received kudos from Malefic in the aggressive behavior categories. Sam never thought of harming himself or others. He never fantasized about murder. He wasn't the type who could imagine himself doing it. He never fantasized or realized anything like that. He never clenched his fist in anger and there was none in his heart. He hated most people and most people hated him. According to Malefic, Sam thought of himself and acted in the realm where he was no good but that so was everybody else. Eight-hours every day, however, he was different. He showed another side of himself. He showed his good side and as a result he became useful to *Me*.

Sam's guilt free zone was his thievery as a teenager. He never paid homage to violence because he never dealt with evil, not for a second, according to Malefic's report.

Malefic provided another path. If only the person knew that they were being tested. Maybe, they'd think differently. If he took the path, he was toast.

The third interrogation followed up three weeks later. This time, Manuel was arrested. Jackson led his team to bring him in. He sat in the same seat, in the same interrogation room. He was very relaxed before. He was free of any criminal jewelry. But, today, he wore handcuffs behind his back. Manuel's mood and demeanor was quite different the third time around. Jackson sank his teeth into him. The evidence became the club which the detective used to bludgeon him. Manuel looked more defiant than he was defeated at first. The amount of evidence that they lacked, and they hoped to find was, finally, compiled into one big giant punch in Manuel's gut. He listened for an hour as Jackson screamed at him about all the evidence. The detective's manner was so harsh, Manuel began to cry with his chin on his chest. Whether the sociopath felt anything but pity for himself was unknown. He, eventually, lifted his head and started to talk. He confessed, but his story changed over the weeks and months; he was less culpable because of his mental health and abuse. I never knew for sure that a person with mental illness, for the most part, knew the difference between right and wrong, except when their mind is in the throes of psychosis. If the individual was sick with it, they were insane. But evil was certainly not insane. And this was just plain evil.

A trial followed because of Manuel's plea, despite his confession. He changed his plea from guilty to not guilty by reason of insanity. The jury took only a few hours until they reached a verdict. Manuel stood with his head down. He heard the words. Sam knew that he was on antipsychotic medication, which was new. He was only diagnosed and treated for depression before. The killer had gone misdiagnosed since childhood. Manuel received the kind of important resources from Lily that Frank never provided for Boris. Yet they both landed themselves in the worst position a human must tolerate. He was sent to prison. He received no allowance for being underage. In fact, it led, very early on, for Manuel to fight for his manhood. He stemmed from pure machismo. He protected himself from sexual assault so many times that it got to the point that he, for a month, stayed in solitary confinement.

Sam never visited Manuel. Manuel's uncle never exchanged email. Sam was the absent uncle. Just like Uncle Stu was to Sam. Lily had her hands full. Sam should've connected more with them, and that sort of thing was what bothered him most: his inability to connect with family or any normal people. Sam didn't beat mental illness, he fought it. It won most of the time. Sam had resigned himself to what occurred. His sister, Lily, was the only soul, besides his grandparents, that he ever felt anything for.

Chapter 2

Sam flew back to Las Vegas. Pearl needed a small pet-carrier. Malefic understood that Sam was incapable of doing anything for himself, which he believed at the time. M-workers enlisted two men who assisted without Sam asking. They, really, did all the work as Sam watched. Pearl was such a gentle dog, but she was also stubborn. Sam never feared that she was vicious. He departed the plane with Pearl in one bag. He had the marijuana too; it was checked in, and there were no problems.

A few weeks passed before he got a letter from the VA. He was to meet with a private psychologist who contracted with VA. She interviewed Sam, regarding his service-connected disability. When he left her office that day the psychologist estimated that it might be a six-month wait. They had to do a deep dive to make that determination.

Six months passed, then seven, eight and nine; nothing. One day, in the tenth month, Sam received two envelopes: He presumed that one announced their decision. The other; it was from the U.S. Treasury. He was approved and the amount of money he received changed Sam's life. It also kindled him. It started a small flame that reignited a symptom of his bipolar. He spent a lot of money; no gambling; not one penny.

After he had lost, virtually, every possession to that guy on the island in Washington. While Sam was in the hospital he got a call from him. He told Sam that if he didn't come for his possessions within the week his stuff would be thrown out. Sam told him that he would come for them, but he never did. He abandoned it all. Frankly, he didn't care as much after he received his VA disability because everything that he left behind on that island were possessions that he always "traveled" with. He never missed any of it. He didn't have any clothing but that was quickly resolved.

Sam never knew when Gilbert placed the ad. His future landlord renovated an old motel from the 1930s. It was on the market for decades. There were nine-suits. One room had the kitchen and living room. The other was the bedroom and the bathroom. The rooms were perfect for Sam and Pearl, it was also very affordable. Gilbert didn't want a pet deposit, which most other rentals did, especially in an apartment community. The town sat along the rugged Pacific coast. There were about five thousand people, ten thousand dogs and thirty-six thousand birds.

Everything changed for Sam and Pearl. But, before they arrived at Sam's newest location, he drove over one-thousand miles from Nevada up to Washington, two very strange occurrences happened. The first night Sam and Pearl slept in the truck. Mr. Miles, as he called himself once, drove nearly thirty-thousand miles and he never, ever slept in the car. He was flush with money from the VA, yet he did not get a hotel room. He and Pearl slept in the car. Sam never thought through what happened; it was unnecessary and crazy. Covid was at full strength. Maybe, it was Malefic, the M-workers didn't want Sam to catch the deadly virus.

At five o'clock in the morning Sam got back on the highway. He drove for two-hours, and he was dazed. He saw a sign. A sign pointed him to the location. So he made a right and he made his way up a mountain. Picture rocks-sized softballs on an unpaved road that snaked around the side of it. Immediately, Sam spoke to Pearl. "Oh, my God," that's how scared he was but he kept going, and he continued: "Oh, my God." There was snow on the mountain. There were no other cars or people. When he looked to his left he must have been up three-thousand feet. As it started to snow he attempted to back the vehicle up. He attempted the maneuver to go back down the nightmarish mountain pathway. He never turned the pick-up truck around. His back tire was stuck in a ditch in the mud. There was no way out. We were three-thousand feet up the side of a mountain as it snowed. There was no cell phone service.

Sam got out of the truck once. He thought he'd walk down the mountain's rocky road to get help. He never made it. It snowed so hard that he walked about five minutes and determined that it was not safe; he couldn't make it. M-workers issued a warning, which transmitted a red alert to him, that if he went any further he was in trouble because M-workers introduced a thought that said: "If you fall, you will not get up." He turned around and sincerely struggled to get back as twilight approached.

Sam and Pearl spent the night there. The dimwitted driver turned on the engine every twenty-minutes to warm up the cab. He was soaked by the snow. The car's heater dried his clothes. The next morning, he thought that he needed to try again. The only way to get help was to go down the mountain. It was around ten o'clock, and the sky was clear. Suddenly, he heard an engine. He kicked open the passenger side door. It was another vehicle. The man worked for the county and he came up to measure the snowpack. The saviour pointed to an area and told the stranded citizen that he once found a dead person in a car. The rooted man looked at Sam's situation. The miracle worker pulled Sam and Pearl out. The good samaritan turned the truck around for Sam.

Pearl and I went down the side of the mountain quickly thereafter. Sam never knew the man's name, but he thanked him very much. But what the County Worker did, Sam thought, was the beginning of his awareness that something consistently happened to him. *Something saved him from danger and trouble too many times.*

Chapter 3

Pat's alcoholism and her Pliartrum drug addiction took a turn for the worse; she was arrested on a DUI. When she worked, she drank and smoked. So, when she got into her car and drove home every night; it was bound to happen. Frank bailed her out. When Sam went to Boris' sentencing hearing, she looked ill. Frank looked embarrassed to be there.

Boris appeared in an orange jumpsuit and chains as he entered the courtroom. The teen looked less defiant. He was born Boris Karloff Isaac. Frank told his older brother it was "so cool to pick out a newborn's name." He felt that he honored Boris by giving him the name. "It did," according to Pat. They watched old horror movies from the 1930s and 40s together when he was young. "Frankenstein, The Bride of Frankenstein, and the Son of Frankenstein were honored movies in the household.

Boris was a difficult child to raise." He was born unwanted which impacted the family nucleus. He was ignored more than he was loved. As a teen he was disciplined and punished almost daily. He was rarely rewarded with something. Frank and Pat raised him like they were raised. They expected him to succeed, but he skirted their expectations. He dropped out of high school in the tenth grade. "But he earned his GED," she defended. The boy stood taller than Frank, who was six-feet-three inches. He was good looking, and the girls liked him. So, something went wrong in Doctor Frankenstein's laboratory, Sam thought.

When Sam "traveled" he always made a stop at Frank's. They put Sam in the extra bedroom once. He stayed in the notorious basement every other time. In total there were five trips of Sam as he "traveled" over forty years. In the cellar, his cluster headaches and depression were very bad. One night, he had another cluster headache. He had nothing to fight it with. In addition, his lower back went out, and he had to pee. It was all at the same time. Pinned to the floor he dragged himself to the bathroom. Without doubt, it could have won the prize as the worst experience in his whole life. One day, in the morning, when he was in the guest room, Sam heard through his closed bedroom door the struggle between an addicted mother and her dysfunctional son. Pat said things like: "If you don't go to school then you can't have any dessert tonight. I made an apple pie." He retorted: "I don't care. I don't want to go to school." Frank and Pat were pushed to the limit and attended a few emergency parent/teacher conferences over the years. The father always told the boy: "I never, in my life, had a parent/teacher conference; emergency or not."

When they lived out in Patriot Park, Pat told Sam that Boris liked to trap small rodents with a cardboard box. One year, Frank bought him a small trap for his birthday. The main problems that Boris had centered around Frank, and his inept parenting. Frank's indifference, Pat's alcoholism, along with her use of Pliartrum's drugs, created the perfect storm. They were too loose with Boris. He was allowed to run roughshod in the home. Frank told him: "when you were a youngster a disturbed stork brought you to us." The misshapen mind believed it. When he got older the "philosopher," said one day: "I don't like being human. I'd rather have been a part of the bird or lizard world; he said that it would be "real cool to be a vulture or a Komodo Dragon."

Boris faced the music that day. It lasted more than an hour. It took place in the same courtroom where he was tried and found guilty. The kid faced the death penalty or life in prison without parole. Sam talked to him about it. Because his mother and father never did, since the guilty verdict. Frank never loved him following his childhood years before the age of ten. Sarah was off at college. She was in her freshman year, studying to be a nurse, something she always wanted to be. And Pat, she was drowning in alcohol.

Sam's presence, at the sentencing hearings, helped nothing. Boris's eyes looked defiant. The Honorable Judge who rose above him entered, which followed the Bailiff's announcement. Everyone, except Boris, stood until the judge took his seat and gaveled in. The court sentencing allowed different family and friends, who were believably broken-hearted, over the manner of their loved one's deaths. For people who died because of natural causes, or even after a long illness; it was easier to cope with. When murdered, everyone who knew the victim felt horrible for her, and themselves as if it had happened to them.

Boris was still slouched at his Defense Council's table. His head darted like a dog. He was flanked by his attorney, a public defender. The prosecutor sat adjacent to the defense. Sam sat in the courtroom crowded by the press, family and friends of the deceased.

Sam thought about it. It sent his mind back to the time he watched the full interrogation of Boris online. Detective Wicks was fantastic. He circled the boy like he was a giant anaconda, and it wrapped around its prey before he went in for the kill. He stroked the boy's ego from the second he walked into that interrogation room. He soon got him to talk. The detective told Boris:

"Wow! You're confident, cool, and unique. Where did you obtain the knowledge to do all of this? Were you watching stuff?"

"No," Boris replied, "the knowledge just comes to me." He went on: "I've developed myself as an assassin."

"Did you have training?" he asked the boy.

"No, it was from my imagination," he replied.

"Where did you get the knife?" Wicks inquired

"From my Aunt Glenda," he said.

The Judge looked like a learned man. His white hair and low brow fit the ambiance. He sat down and read paperwork. Family and friends of the victim took the stand. One member presented their soul to the Court in place of the beloved woman who was of very old age. "Take me," she cried. Boris shook his head, Sam remembered.

The Prosecution's recommendations were firm: death. "Is the public defender prepared to argue?"

The lawyer, basically, argued that Boris presented a danger to society but that his life should be spared because he's a juvenile. Capital Punishment rarely happens to a minor in the US, but it's happened.

"When she became pregnant; she wanted the child; it was the father who didn't. But Frank did the right thing. After she became pregnant, they married. There was always a conflict between the father and the son; it only became worse as he aged. When he was born, he was a burden in his father's eyes. So, when it came to parenting," the Public Defender explained, "financially, they spent little on the boy; he went without. Clothes, dentist, doctors, haircuts; it all added up.

Boris was neglected in his early years. The father took his frustrations out of the boy. The mother's love was too weak to overcome the powerful developmental punishment of the child by the parents. The father thought that he was just doing the right thing when he took on the role of Dad. But he never, really, wanted the part. He never shook away from his responsibility for producing the child. The young killers' mind was a piece of clay, and it was a misshapen mess. The parents never lifted a finger. Finances weren't spent on him. They only took him to the dentist once. The boy never received instructions. He was left to figure out life on his own. His goodness and other important aspects of it went undeveloped, as a result. You want to, really, know what went wrong with my client, just turn on the television, or go to a movie or just hop on the Internet. Disturbing messages and images are being sent to their fertile minds every second of every day."

"The defendant will rise," the judge said. Boris stood.

The Judge cleared his voice. "The jury has found you guilty in the murder of Betty Laslo, in the first degree with malice. I understand the defendant has something to say before I rule."

The Defender looked at Boris for a second. "Your Honor, I realize that I'm here for you to impose my punishment. All I can say is that it's hard." Boris turned around with contempt written all over his face he bellowed. "Fuck you."

The Judge gaveled in, several times, as the uniformed court personnel, two junior staffers, took action. Boris was physically returned to his seat. Once seated, the court's workhorses remained in place with their hands on the shoulders of the defendant. The Judge read from his prepared remarks. "The defendant has not convinced this court that he understands the gravity of his actions." He looked up and said: "Your latest outburst only strengthens that finding. You're a very ill, young man. But you knew right from wrong, and, yet you pursued the wrong. I find no extenuating circumstances. "Boris Karloff Isaac, having been found guilty of this heinous crime, I sentence you to death."

Boris lifted his arm far enough, and he gave the Judge the finger. The wise man ignored him. He struck the gavel, rose, and left the courtroom.Sam watched Boris as the two courthouse law enforcers lifted him out of his seat; each had a hold of an arm, and they led him away. He dragged his legs, so they were forced to lift him. He smiled on his way out. His expression reminded Sam of *Norman Bates* at the end of the film: *"Psycho."*

Chapter 4

Frank told Sam the young killer wrote to him. He said that he found religion and espoused Pliartrumism. Frank never pitied the boy, "they were just words," he said. Then he insulted Sam because, he said, of his constant rants and how dangerous Pliartrum was. Again, Sam feared not, and he amplified his support for Lily, and the People Party, and his hatred for Pliartrum and the Country Club Party.

Later, Sam realized that Malefic was up to its normal antics. It created conflict in the world, so often, over mankind's existence, it's countless. But I understood why. Exactly, what happened to America during Pliartrum's terms in Office was all courtesy of Malefic, because the Country, just like Germany, of the 1930s, followed the Pied Piper right into the river of raw sewage.

It was years ago. But, "however many years later," I told him, "this country is resilient; it always has been," I said, "the American people should've never allowed organized crime to get their foot into the door of the Federal Government in the first place; but the mob and its allies hoodwinked the people "Pliartrum was kin to the most evil force in the Universe." That his words were rooted in the Nazism and Satanism.

"Under Pliartrum, the US suffered," I pronounced to Frank's defiant eyes, "his four-years in the White House, and his "post-presidency, and now his current term" told it all. I said, "it didn't matter what happened next. The damage had been done. America would never be the same because of Pliartrum, his family, friends, those political and non-political hacks, and all of his merry goons who supported, aided and abetted his criminality. It was just like the time that he built that retreat/casino. The mob had it built, they milked it dry, and it went into bankruptcy. When he took the Oval Office, there was a photo taken by the Russian media, the US media were denied access, but, even so, the photo generated much more than a thousand words. It was more like a million. Polar Trump was in cahoots with Russia.

Pliartrum robbed the Treasury; and crippled the IRS. He destroyed the Justice Department, and hobbled homeland security. He wanted to dismantle NATO. The idiot president placed the country's intelligence and law enforcement entities, namely, the FBI, CIA, NTF, as well as the Secret Service, into grave danger. The organized crooks took control of the Federal Government; it was like magic to Pliartrum. The Federal government, however, was in grave danger if, God forbid, Pliartrumism continued. He was in bed with all the crooks of the World, he always was. They and Pliartrum aimed for glory. They expected, insisted and instituted organized crime like methods and practice, with the goal of World domination. Pliartrum wanted to be the World's first trillionaire.

Lily wrote in her comment on YouTube: *Don't let organized crime rule America.* Sam thought about it and decided that she should've added: *Don't let organized crime rule the World.* "They want to make the United States an oligarchical system, just like Russia. Washington, D.C. would be called "little Moscow," he wrote in a comment left on a Youtube video and Sam set up a website called: Lily's Lane. He reposted everything she ever wrote. Pliartrum, once again, was given word of it. Lily was dead but Sam Isaac was still alive.

People like Lily and Sam stood up for Democracy and the Constitution. They were against authoritarianism and mob-rule economy. Their feet were planted. They held the signs at demonstrations that were on the side of peace and tolerance, and against Pliartrum, hate and organized crime.

Chapter 5

The new song the girls collaborated on was "very nice," according to Cathy's Mom. As young Sherman played her melody on the piano, Sarah sang the lyrics that she wrote. They planned to upload it on YouTube. Doctor and Mrs. Sherman had their coats on when they entered the den. "We're ready to leave." The moment was captured by M-watchers. The M-team posted notice that M-workers would, soon, be rotated. All hands were on deck in Malefic's world. Sarah, usually, walked back and forth between her home and Cathy's. That day, in the late afternoon, Doctor Sherman offered Sarah a ride. They were going past her home. The young teen shrugged her shoulders and said: "okay." Cathy and Sarah sat in the back. The doctor's daughter asked her mother if Sarah could come with them. They were to attend a play at the community theater. Their nephew, the son of the doctor's brother, starred in a musical called: *Annie Get Your Gun.* The doctor received three tickets from the young-teen and promised that they would be there for opening night. The theater was sold-out, according to Mrs. Sherman. Cathy and Sarah planned to meet the next day.

As Pat ran the vacuum cleaner in the basement. The mother of two said that she never heard a thing, but the doctor claimed that after the accident every neighbor looked out their door or window. Frank's house sat on a street that had some traffic in the daytime. The street was broad enough that another bank of homes sat opposite Frank's house. It was a two-way street, but it was residential, and the speed limit was twenty-five miles per hour. When the Doctor slowed, pulled over, and put his foot on the brake, Sarah's M-team faced its toughest assignment. The arrangement for the death of a very good person. It always meant the M-teams coordinated the accident with each person's M-team involved. Nothing was left to chance. The coordination began days ago. Each life that Sarah touched was affected by it. Wounds to her loved ones that lasted forever.

The time was five minutes before sunset. The sun's glare prompted each front seat occupant to lower their visor. The moment was prepared. M-worker's data showed that all of the parties were in place. The doctor put his flashers on. Sarah, who sat in the back, took off her seatbelt. She unlocked it and she pushed the door open. She got out waving and looking at Cathy. She never saw it coming. She turned to face it a split second before it happened. A car came directly at her. She had no time to act, because it was her expiration date. She was just fourteen, and she died in her mother's arms. After Pat turned off the vacuum she heard her neighbor, who was frantically coming down the basement steps screaming. She went up two-steps at a time to hold her daughter for the last time. When Sam was told of the tragedy Malefic showed how cruel life can be. Her accidental death killed the hope and dreams of not just Sarah that day. Her data played mattered; it touched this earth.

Frank returned from the *J6* that Pliartrum ordered. The president's unspeakably selfish act placed many lives onto pathways that they never had been on before. The sizable number of people gathered at the capital Frank watched from afar. His phone vibrated as he was walking back to the bus. "His face turned white," according to one friend that was there.

The consequences of a child's death, especially by accident, were profound. The doctor, his wife and Cathy never arrived at the play that night. Sarah was pronounced dead at the scene by Doctor Sherman. The Shermans stayed with Pat, who needed consoling, until Frank came home. The Shermans consoled the couple for hours. "We sat on the sofa and side chairs in the living room." Pat told Sam that Frank collapsed when we all stood to say good-bye. After the door was closed, Frank, who the doctor helped revive, sat on the sofa. As his hands gripped his head. The pain in his face was palpable. He lowered his torso into his lap.

The funeral was very sad, Sam's data showed. He stood amongst dozens of young teens and their parents. Sam, finally, was placed into retirement by Malefic. He lived on the other side of the country, and when he arrived, in his hometown, the next day. Pat told Sam that Frank would not allow me into his house, so I stayed at a hotel.

Chapter 6

Politics aside, goodness was never far from our hearts. Good people tolerated a lot. They don't agree a lot of the time. People became more tolerant of others in the last century. Outright hatred from these little anti-boy scouts with guns was like the Nazi party in the 1930s. They got their boot into the door of the Chancellery, and it's all history from there.

Malefic's lesson was, apparently, not learned, hence, our current dilemma. What harm this disease, this scourge, this Pliartrum caused for this country, its people, its institutions, families, friendships and communities, and it's all for one simple reason: greed and power. Organized Crime got their foot in the door when Pliartrum was nominated for the Country Club Party in 2016. Now, it's solidified. Organized crime was very happy about their newest enterprise and they were not about to give it up so easily.

He was only an organized crime player up to that point. Once he sat in the Oval Office Slowly during term one, but it gushed out upon his second bite of the apple. Organized crime crept into the Federal system. Everything in the candy store was up for grabs. The Federal Government was like a tinkertoy when they first muscled their way into the arteries and veins, and into the fabric of this Land. Lily warned Sam, and she was right. She'd be amazed to learn that her comment on YouTube contributed to the exposure of Pliartrum as the simple mob-thug that he always was. "That one attribute, thug criminality, entered the Lexicon in the 1970s, we became a nation that idolized it," according to Lily. "There were gangsters, long ago, people watched, on the silver screens before television, and it wasn't a big deal; it never entered our Lexicon.

Then came the cultural side effects of the remarkable films, by Francis Ford Coppola about the mob. Everyone wanted in on it. The movies and television fed the masses great stories where the bad guys won. Pliartrum in those days admired mob bosses, and when he became of use to them, he became a player. His father's wealth separated young Rich Pliartrum from the average street thug. But Pliartrum, through Malefic, lived out his fantasy. The lane was created long ago. It's a lane for the very few. It always led to disaster for good people around the world. These teeny-weeny brains, like Pliartrum, Hitler and even back to Ivan the Terrible, always fizzled out and were destroyed. The destruction that took place led to peace and tranquility for a hundred-years. World War I and World War II taught mankind a lesson, which was learned. Evil was defeated and peace prevailed, despite cool relations between the US and Soviet Union. No wars were raging on European soil until Tutin supremely screwed up. Pliartrum's mouth watered when he realized that the Russian leader had bitten off more than he could chew in his invasion into a neighboring country.

A year passed, Sam exchanged emails with Pat, but he remained canceled in Frank's culture. Pat spent a lot of time at the Legion that year. The absence of offspring impacted their relations. They each had a separate life. Neither visited Boris on the death row.

When I heard that Frank planned a *J6* party, marking its first anniversary, on the very day that his daughter was killed, a year before, I felt his psychosis. The day was to be the unveiling of Sarah's headstone. That afternoon, I ate at a fast-food restaurant while the rest of the family was gathered in Frank's basement for a stand-up catered affair which followed the unveiling. Glenda, who did enter Frank's house, after bitching about it for decades, along with Uncle Stu both stood amongst Frank's *J6* - Bubba crew, who all brought their wives and girlfriends. The upper echelon smiled and nodded to the lower leveled individuals. They were two different breeds of people sharing the same common interest: their support for Pliartrum. My upper-class family members were impeccably dressed. Frank got back into his jeans, as Pat and her friends prepared for the party. The dress-code called for jeans and t-shirts; Pliartrum t-shirts, of course. Frank had a dozen in a box in the basement's utility room.

Fifty people gathered that night. Frank went all out. Tiki-torches, ablaze, were placed ten-feet apart around the perimeter of the chain link fence. The swimming pool was covered by a quarter of an inch layer of ice. and the lights of the watering hole were turned on. There were three groups, some were just for the guys and some were just for the gals. The rest mingled amongst them. The handful of men talked as they gossiped and consumed alcohol from its containers.

Sam didn't go to the catered lunch because he wasn't invited. He waited until that night to go to Frank's J6 - one year anniversary party. There was a time when Sam, without doubt, should've never come to a social gathering. Especially a Pliartrum one. Sam's seethed nerves prickled when he consumed any of their poison, even for a second. But something happened. It happened before. He was used to it by now. Malefic choreographed a marvelous dance for Sam and the Pliartrum's faithful. The M-team and Malefic served Sam too many times for him to count. Malefic had a service for Sam to perform. You might say that he was in rehearsal for sixty-years, and now, Malefic revealed his purpose to himself. It was hard to imagine that after all of these decades, his help from Malefic was to be repaid in the 21st Century, and after all that time, it came to me, Frank and his friends. None of the regular neighbors that I knew from when I "traveled," were present. These people were brought to face myself. I, in turn, was brought to face Malefic. It enforced the Executives' POV. Summoned, Malefic carried out orders. Directives that changed societies, forever.

Chapter 7

When Sam walked through the gate, it took just seconds to hear Frank yell: "What are you doing? Why are you here? Keith spoke up and said:

"He's brainwashed by the People's Party."

Sam looked hurt when he heard their laughter. Chance piped up and yelled:

"Yeah, we want to kill the People's Party. Pliartrum has all of you ready for the ovens." Guests hooped and hollered. Frank remained silent. The music from the outdoor speakers stopped and so did everybody else. Sam thought that he, once again, stood in front of a classroom of elementary school children. Kids were frozen by their M-workers to open up all channels to receive important Malefic content.

They looked like a mean bunch but Sam had taken over classrooms in his days as a substitute teacher, which were deemed uncontrollable according to the teacher's note to the substitute. "Call for the principal if the student, whose desk was up against the chalkboard, acts out." One fourth grader was a scattered mess. Her hair was pulled out in patches; she had done it. She took her seat. The rest of the class did the same. Sam never talked about the fact that he had passed on to children, ever since he improved his life, information for the development of the soul. Sam no longer felt that he was hated when he first started working as a substitute teacher. He was welcomed and respected now, and it was all due to Malefic's words. Sam said: Before he never took credit for someone else's work. However, they even impacted on the students who had all the problems. She, and the rest of the class, presented no problems that day. Sam's note to the teacher was that the students did well today. The kicker, however, was three-weeks later, when Sam was at the same school again. He supervised the kids who were on the playground for lunch period. As he stood there the fourth-grade girl, who had all the problems, ran up to him and said: "I wanted to thank you, Mister Isaac, you taught me how to be good." As she walked away, Sam realized that the words in the shower that day, way back when, were magical.

Their impressionable eyes yearned for information. Sam provided it when he stood in front of a classroom filled with kids. They were light hearted words that carried a lot of weight.

"Everybody has a good side to them and a bad side, and when you come to school you need to show your good side. You need to show it to your teacher. You need to show it to your fellow classmates, and you need to show it to yourself. Because you need to be aware that it's there, because your good side is a very important part of you, and you need to bring it out and use it! When we're at home our brothers and sisters, or someone shows us their bad sides, and we turn right around, and show them ours. It's an automatic reflex just like when the doctor hits your knee with a little rubber hammer your leg will always pop up. But you're not at home, you're at school, and so you've got to act differently. What do you think that your mom and dad would do if they went to work, and they were silly and goofy, or they were mean or mad. What do you think would happen to them if they did that? "They'd be fired, " was their answer. Sam agreed with them and added -- so, school is a very important place. And when we are in public, which means that we're not at home. This is your job. You are a student and you'll have this job for many years, and then you'll have a grown-up job just like a grown-up. So, when you come to school, show your good

side: when we show our good side, good things happen to us. When we show our bad side, bad things happen. So, when you find yourself in an important place, it's important to show your best. Never your worst."

As the tiki torch lights beamed and bounced off the thin layer of ice covering the pool. All eyes were on Sam, and to him they were red with fire in them. But, suddenly, he felt warmth in his eyes, and he knew why: Malefic. Sam never saw children's expressions so eager to watch, listen, and learn.

However, when Sam showed up, on that day the power in their eyes at the party reminded the unwanted guest of the power of evil. Not the power of goodness. Sam hadn't seen that since he was a boy, and he looked at black and white photos of World War II. They were ordinary Germans and they were swallowed up by the Nazis, who carried the power of hate and they became Nazi too. They spread it throughout the land. Nobody was immune to it. It was either to be a good Nazi or else.

Malefic revealed knowledge, to Sam, just bits at a time. He witnessed how Malefic's words impacted unruly young kids in a classroom, but Sam wasn't so sure he could grab and keep the attention of those that surrounded him on that very night. Alcohol was the main fuel that generated the party goers, as each held a bottle of beer in their hand. In one swoop, those gathered were taken aback. Sam looked at Frank and he was stunned. Pat was too. They were all stunned. Just like in school. Just like in Sam's last MH job when he presented words that came to him, and that he wrote down.

The pool was ringed by Pliartrum's people. They looked at Sam with contempt. He, for that moment, felt that he held their attention. These were, exactly, the kinds of people who he needed to reach. Good people who've latched on to evil, Pliartrum. It's not their fault. It's happened many times before in history, it's a powerful spell that they were under. Sam tried to reach Frank; he stopped talking to me. The brothers haven't spoken for five-years now. And it's all because of one man. Sam had a message for him and the others gathered. As his eyes moved around the perimeter of the pool, Uncle Stu and Glenda came out of the house. They held mixed drinks. They were dressed up like it was a swanky affair. With jaws dropped they stared, and it seemed as if they moved in slow-motion as they joined the others around the chlorinated watering hole of frozen H2O, they just continued staring at Sam like he was a bug in a mason jar. The M-workers were ordered into full conflict mode. They played both sides. However, M-watchers very rarely interfered in these types of human interaction. The amount of data that was generated by these types of incidents determined that it was a life changing event. Each player's M-teams connected. Malefic's motive was the same it's been since the first brother against brother occurred. Cain slew Abel, and it's never stopped since.

Sam never thought, for one second, that his school pitch to kids would be effective on followers of Pliartrum, so he began by saying: "We are all being tested. We are tested as children and as teenagers. We are tested as individuals when we move forward with our lives as adults. We're tested each moment of each day."

One guest spoke up: "Who gives a fuck. Everybody remained silent. Sam never hesitated. "Malefic is what it's called. We're puppets on its strings. It's testing us. It provided pathways to carry out our wishes we hold close to the heart. Our society. Us as individuals, from birth to death, are tested. Every interaction we have with ourselves, and others produces data, it's given to Malefic. It gives it to the Executives, Jesus, Mohammed and Buddha, who presents it to God, it's that crucial.

"Go to Hell," one voice said..

"It's to gauge our morality. We are slowly evaporating. We're going backwards instead of forward in time. And all that mankind gained over the fifty-sixty years, in civil rights, women's rights, all kinds of rights for the protection of people and animals alike are gone; poof. People learned that they had the right to live freely without harassment. To be cordial and civil when we're in public. Malefic, probably, understands when we act out at home behind closed doors. If you hate people, you're wrong. Do you, for one second, think that God, or your Executive wants you to hate your fellowman? Hitler wanted Germans to do that, and they did it. Now there's Pliartrum and he asks for the same exact things that Hitler wanted and tried to get away with, but he didn't and neither will Pliartrum.

Tragedy breeds tragedy and with all the little rats who were pardoned, and released, soon after he took office. J6 demonstrated to Sam that Pliartrum and Tutin must be fought, just like Hitler and Mussolini in WWII. Sam was prepared to carry on Lily's work. When he served in the military a long war had just ended. He used to think, mistakenly, that his service to the country went awry, because he never appreciated the democracy that he lived in and served as a seaman. Those were carefree days in the military. Somehow, history never mattered in the latter half of the 1970s. But Pliartrum changed how he felt. He posted a response to Lily's comment, and now, she was no longer alive to fight for it. He took her place in my mind. And he was determined to fight Pliartrum. He sensed a shift in the gathered group, and a few guys met off to the side. Sam finished with the thought: "Do you want an America where the thugs are in charge? Well, I don't!" Frank and his crew who stood behind Sam pulled him away from where he stood. They put him on the ground. Each took one of his limbs. They swung Sam back and forth three times before they hurled him into the water. The ice broke up. The J6 party erupted. Sam's jaw dropped. In a frozen state he looked at his arms and hands. As Sam scurried to an edge of the pool to grab hold. Only one person came to help him: Pat. S.When it all started.she was inside with 30 more party goers and she was drunk. Ever since Sarah's death she drank more and more. As the commotion continued she went outside with 30 others who quickly followed. She witnessed the very moment Sam was hoisted into the pool icy water. Pat helped pull him out. But

Sam's dead weight only brought her into the water too. Everyone, but the two in the pool, laughed, hooted, hollowered, and clapped their hands.

Chapter 8

After Lily's horrific death Sam vowed to pick up her political mantle so that he and other good hearted people continued the fight against Pliartrum. He started by creating a website in 2022 and it was called: "Horace Pliartrum for President." The site was dedicated to the president's nephew Horace, a psychiatrist by trade. Sam wrote 12 blogs and maintained the site for a year but nobody ever visited it. The blogs were supposed to explain why Horace would be better than Rich. Soon after the 2024 election, however, he was concerned about his safety.

Sam's gut told him that he might be on the president's enemies list because of Lily's comment which he reposted using his Youtube account on the eve of President Pilartrum's reelection victory. Pliartrum's response and his veiled personalized threat he issued to Lily, now applied to him because of what he wrote but he was never on social media and as a result Pliartrum never had a chance for his people to troll him. Sam commented on every Pliatrum's related video and there thousands with Lily's original warning about Pliatrum and organized crime. Sam was crushed when he won. He was convinced that the democratic candidate would win. It wasn't close; however, he beat his opponent by 7 million votes.

Pliartrum II went far beyond his first term in office. The president was now in the position to make himself and many others disgustingly rich. It seems they never had enough. They wanted more. He started his second term thievery with the crown jewels of this nation: the Constitution. Everyday he issued a new outrage; it was like Pliartrum created the office: Owning the Libs, and each morning the first thing Pliartrum looked for was a report of who was hit and how they were punished. The report also indicated who was next on the long list, an outline of each crime against Pliartrum by those targeted for that day, along with punishments recommendations compiled by OOT. It didn't take long for Pliartrum to set up his retribution teams. Recruited by the administration were men and women from the CIA, ICE, and ATF.

It was around that time that a series of unbelievable events took place in Sam's life. He took Peart on a walk to the beach everyday and one day a pleasant scent was present in the air. Sam inhaled it deeply, and as a result, because it was pollen, he developed a sinus infection. For the next three months it was all downhill. He was treated for fluid retention; he lost 15 pounds in one day. Also, he had to have a pacemaker put in because of low blood pressure. One day, soon after the pacemaker was put in, he was in the parking lot outside his $800/mo apartment, and he fainted. Seconds later he was conscious and bleeding from the head. He was rushed to the emergency room where he received ten stitches.

The emergency room doctor sewed Sam up, but because the pacemaker was put in only a week ago she wanted him to go inpatient that night so that the next day the cardiology people could assess if there was a problem with the pacemaker..

That day came and went, and two men from cardio slid their testing machine by Sam's bedside and the determined that there was no problem. The next day Sam's doctor stood at the foot of his hospital bed and said: "We're going to discharge you tomorrow." That day came and went. Sam's was being held and the hospital kept him hospitalized for 10 days. Officially, it was charted that he was in a state of delirium. However, what really happened was that one of Pliartrum's retribution teams was dispatched after the government put a hold on his discharge.

Sam was drugged and tortured a variety of ways over the seven-day period. They used a drug that resulted in Sam having double vision, every word he uttered he stuttered, and he couldn't stand. The report said that Sam kept saying: "All I ever did was comment on a YouTube video."

The team remained silent as they put Sam through a series of what can only be described as low grade torture. First they moved him into an MRI machine, and they turned the levels as high as could go, surpassing the safety range. This caused tremendous pain over the 20 minutes he was inside the machine. During the torture session someone on the team had the machine send out pulses of pain every 20 seconds. Sam was constantly drugged and guarded during those days. On the fourth day Sam was not allowed to urinate. Three of the men would not allow him to stand to pee in the plastic bottle yet alone use the bathroom. Every time Sam tried to get up they set him back down. He retained enough fluids that a catheter was installed and he quickly filled the bag. The next day Sam refused to eat or drink. On day five, however, the government agents placed a breathing mask over his mouth and nose. As Sam breathed his ribs were, one at a time, slowly going back and forth and consequently breaking. They broke five ribs in all.

The way Sam figured it Pliartrum's possy got word of him when he went inpatient. Each new patient was entered into the database and Pliartrum's people moved exponentially. In retrospect Sam wasn't sure but the government thugs may have tried to get to him when he was hospitalized before but they were unable to get there in time because he only stayed two-nights and was discharged. When Sam appeared on their radar again they moved quickly. First a representative from Pliartrum's team called the hospital and spoke to someone in authority. The call, with some cover story, was to place a hold on Sam.

A man fainted. His head injury required 10 stitches. Most people enter the hospital sick or injured and leave feeling better. The patient felt well enough to go home and the doctor was in agreement. But with Sam after six-days being under the thumb of Pliartrum's retribution squad they went away but he couldn't stay there because he didn't trust anybody. So, Sam went A.M.A. (Against Medical Advice) and he was discharged. It wasn't long before 911 was called again because he was still light headed and dizzy, and was in constant pain after his ribs were broken. Sam called those 10 stitches, once removed and were just above his brow, his Pliartrum scar.

Somehow, later on, Sam wondered if it was Malefic who produced this because the countdown had begun.

EPILOGUE

Lily wanted to change every heart in America. Uncle Stu wanted his Country Club Party in power with Pliartrum at its helm again. Pliartrum fancied himself the most powerful man in history. Pliartrum, Jr. saw himself as his father's successor. Glenda fits right in with all the grifting and the greed. Boris hoped for a reprieve. Frank was more radical than ever, as his social media indicated. Pat, for all practical purposes, was sidelined from alcoholism and her Pliartrum narcotic. Manuel was a different story. His crime horrified me, as did Boris. They were like two tropical storms in the Gulf of Mexico. Correction: The "Gulf of America" as Pliartrum put it. They met, and they increased in strength by the hour. It became a frenzied category-five hurricane that each, separately, conspired with evil. Each carried it out, and imagined themselves doing, not just once, but often, everyday; they craved it. They planned and acted, both in a murderous rage. Manuel's M-team ordered the M-watchers, and, subsequently, the M-workers said that there was another emergency case.

The Malefic Guide was very clear. Chiseled into stone were laws which governed every case of matricide, patricide or parricide. Collected, deep data, instantaneously moved up the chain. Malefic, in consultation with Executives, made the final call. God's muscle waited for an answer. Whether during horror, just before the act, the soul stopped and turned around. Or that he continued and crept forward with murder in his eyes. Every breath from the potential killer generated deep data. It added up to all the fantasies. Multiplied by what Malefic and the M-team's data showed. It looked bad.

They had merged, and it went straight to heart. The killing was set, and he was ready to go. With his act, two lives were cracked open, one literally. It fed darkness to diabolical evil. Malefic issued approval to proceed based on two factors. One was Lily's history of sacrifice and goodness. The other was what young Manuel planned to do. They were placed on their road to oblivion. One returned to whence she came. The other was stored in a cell. He was isolated from Society. Malefic imposed life. It was meant as a living hell. Manuel became a desperado. He aimed for safety through power; it was futile, however. He was targeted whenever he was in the general population. He attempted suicide in his first year; Malefic would have none of it. Soon he fought like a gladiator with a crude weapon he designed out of a piece of plastic. It landed him in solitary confinement. After he came out; he had fire in his eyes. Eventually, however, he was permitted by his M-workers to join a Hispanic gang for his protection. When he first arrived, he wasn't accepted. Manuel worried. It happened much later, but, eventually, Malefic ordered action from the M-team. All of Manuel's M-team was on alert. In the end, the minor received "protection," he said in an email to Pat. But words meant little to Malefic, people said a lot of things. Most of it was classified as gibberish. He wanted Lily out of his life. He, in the sickest throes of his mental illness, never thought about it; he just did it on impulse. He was connected, only to the worst that was inside of him. He thought that he could get away with it, he never focused on the ramifications to his community, his family, and on himself.

As for Sam, the lessons that he learned, he paid dearly for. He never understood his behavior, but he sorely wanted to. He understood his sexuality. Was it wrong? Yes, for Sam. Not for anyone else. It was wrong just for him. It was the path that he ignored for fifty-years. He never felt love because Malefic ordered that he wasn't supposed to. Ergo, the message that he received, on the balcony, at the Temple, was not a request. He wouldn't do it voluntarily; so, it was imposed upon him. He never knew how he transformed into a mindless, although non-violent, criminal as a youth. He never changed. He couldn't. He committed crimes against other people's intangible assets. Things that never belonged to him, but he took it, again and again. He gave his employer's property away to others; some people who he knew, and others he didn't. He just did it randomly. Hundreds and hundreds of dollars of an employer's goods went unpaid for over all those months he worked there. He never thought about it. He just went on gleefully, oblivious to what he was doing. Therefore, he never understood it or other things like why he had no friends. He tried being a part of society, but he never fit in.

Malefic saw to it, however. Sam was given an important gift. He helped others whose minds needed care and attention like his own. He wasn't perfect at it; he made mistakes. But his service to others all came from the heart. And he learned. Eventually, everything changed for him, but it was only after he received his bipolar diagnosis from the VA. He thanked Malefic. He desperately sought answers that were ultimately revealed to him.

It took time. In the end, Malefic gave and taught everybody something. Boris was supported, publicly, by celebrities and spiritually, by Rabbis. He learned the ways of God. Lily expired from the rage of a sociopath. She, most likely, learned that her kindness backfired. Pat got more heartache on top of her alcoholism and her addiction to Pliartrum's drugs. She learned, the hard way, that people who coped better, with life, fared better. On the other hand, Glenda received good-evil from Malefic; she was protected and encouraged. Uncle Stu learned that he and other Country Club Party members were free people, when they were really Hitlerized. The same power, Malefic, that placed the German people, at that time, under political psychosis, did it again. This time, however, it was the United States of America who Malefic targeted. Finally, there was Pliartrum. He should've learned not to respond to an average citizen's comment on YouTube.

As to Sam's heart, for the first time in his life, he tapped into his personal goodness which came from the heart. He never knew what turned it on and off, however. When he walked through the door of the Meyer's Club, it changed his life. Malefic arranged it. He walked on a very special path but he lost it, eventually, at each of his MH jobs. Later, he understood that it was all planned. He did well for a while after that his own MH worsened, and along with cluster headaches he became a wreck, and he remained so for years before he bounced back; it happened four times in thirty-years.

Lily was different, she never lost her mind. As she grew up, she never crossed anyone. Yet, she became a sacrificial lamb. Manuel's machismo was triggered by events, after which, he craved her death. In his eyes she had wronged him one time too many. Her overprotective parenting lit a powder keg. It was toxic to him, and it was concocted by a mind that accepted and responded to internal stimuli. He had terrible impulse control. He saw himself in motion. He relished the thoughts. The young mind performed his deadly deed. Sam understood, later, that M-planners, M-developers and M-coordinators, in cooperation with M-watchers and M-workers were in sync with Lily's M-team, who, by decree, relinquished Lily's soul, which was covered under the Malefic Guidelines, a policy and procedure manual for all M-team personnel.

M-workers positions required recertification. It followed their last assignment. Lily's M-workers were carefully debriefed when they returned. They learned in training that they had the power to change a person's destiny, like Manuel or Boris, that is, if it fell within Malefic's rules, which were issued from above.

Whatever held each back until the pivotal moment, only Malefic, the Executives and I knew. It was the intent that posted red flags to M-watchers, who knew that the person acted out what they fantasized and desired. Malefic provided the real estate, and the M-workers built the path. His M-team led the individual astray. It was tolerated. Tolerance was a very important human quality, which was impossible for some people to show. It could never be called upon. It came from the heart. There were people who weren't interested in personal growth. They never improved their lot in Malefic's assessment of the data. Or they and their leaders ignored truth and tolerance. Thus, they remained steadfast and ignorant. Sam was one of them when he was younger. He was jammed between two slices of moldy bread, Mom and Dad, who never wanted me. He should've understood, long ago, that he courted immorality, and consciously felt free of guilt because there was something wrong with him. It went on for decades. He, nor anyone else, stopped him. He was free to roam wild, and he continued. He made a complete idiot of himself in the process. It took him back to a moment that he vividly remembered. He was a boy again, and he rode in the car, the one headed for the mall. How, from that moment on, he accepted and believed what he heard on that day, and how it impacted him for the rest of his life.

Mistakenly, Sam learned that cuteness was important. He walked a long way before he realized that he was wrong and that he was lost. His aunt told him that he looked like an angel. He went through his early years with that in mind. It followed him into his teens. Much later, as an adult, he realized that he was completely wrong about a person's look. However, one day when he was the substitute teacher, it only proved that he still had a lot to learn. He was assigned to a third-grade class. Some kids were busy with their pencils and worked at their desks. Others were with Sam in a reading group. They sat on small chairs in a circle. Before they got started one of the kids spoke up and caught everyone's attention. He pointed to the boy next to him and he said to me: "He said you're ugly." It was softball. Sam should've hit it out of the park. Instantaneously, any normal adult would respond with the obvious answer. Especially when it comes from a youngster who should have received a totally different response than the one that the substitute teacher gave to him as a grownup. This was the moment for all of them. Sam failed. He never responded with the correct answer. His presence, unfortunately, delivered the wrong message. The simple truth of the adage that; "*beauty comes from within; it doesn't matter what someone looks like on the outside; it's what's on the inside that counts.*" Instead, he sat there like a fool and replied: "Well, he's entitled to his opinion." He not only missed the softball, Sam struck out. He, instantly, should've spouted out the right answer. Much later, he felt ashamed that he didn't.

Sam's mental health education taught him that people who weren't physically beautiful were often beautiful inside. And some people who were candy to the eyes, were very ugly inside. He was one of them, he concluded. That's how he knew. He crossed many people's paths. His innate goodness surfaced. He worked on it a lot, and he taught it, along with the lesson plan for that day. He was always amazed by it. Simple words that came together; it made such a difference; it always set the right tone.

Those words that came to him in the shower connected with people. People found their goodness, some for the very first time. They brought it out and used it. They showed it to me. They showed it to their fellow classmates. And they showed it to themselves.

Glenda was a perfect example. She was a popular socialite, but Sam knew that she was ugly inside. Something else that was ugly was Pliartrum. He didn't just bad mouth someone who he thought wronged him, he was out for blood. He ordered his Muscle to intimidate his followers and opponents, even the average citizen. Just look at what happened to Sam. They were experienced thugs. But regular American people saw through him. After all, I told Lily: "I saw The Godfather fifty-times." Apparently, Pliartrum believed that nobody knew his dirty little secret. The takeover of America by Organized Crime. Don Corleone, if reported correctly, turned over in his grave at the news. The mob always wanted to buy judges and politicians, to put them in their little pockets. Now they demanded judgeships and political office themselves. Their thievery had no boundaries. Glenda and Uncle Stu saw people like me and Lily as dead meat. On television, one night, a follower at a Pliartrum rally, in a silent second, spoke up and bellowed: "When do I get to use my AR-15 on those bastards?" Pliartrum's crowd hooted, hollered and applauded, enthusiastically, their agreement.

Bubba did that a lot. He hooted and hollered when it was J6. He hooted and hollered Pliartrum's attacks on our institutions, primarily, the Justice Department, the FBI, ATF and other institutions dedicated to catching criminals, like the IRS. These were the same institutions that organized crime feared and who the Federal government fought, every day, to weed them out and place them into prison.

What happened, the mob never thought possible, even in their wildest dreams. The leader of organized crime in America became Pliartrum. All he knew was that he was always right about everything and that he wanted to rip-off the Feds as much as he could.

He was never challenged by anyone in the Country Club Party. Why would they? He did nothing wrong. He took no responsibility for any of his presidential crimes, yet alone the others before and after his first term as president. The guy was a petty crook. He was a b-list celebrity from a washed-up television series. He was defeated, eventually. Glenda learned the hard way too. She got cocky on-air, one night. The PROX NEWS' owner read her emails and texts. They were quite provocative and were reported on. When made public, she lost every sponsor. She was canceled with a ten-minute notice. She lost a lot. Her home outside of New York City, sold. Her penthouse in NYC, sold. Her perks were all canceled too. Malefic played hard at times, with the folks in the Country Club Party. After all, they were on the wrong side of every major issue. It was Malefic who put them there. Why not? Pliartrum alienated, demonized, and fought everything that was good, decent, fair and tolerant. Again, it was Malefic who kept track of their cockeyed ideas and conspiracy theories and theorists.

So, Malefic created the conflict and blinded Pliartrum's people from a mountain of truth. If they only knew that they were being played the whole time. Bubba was the sucker. Evil flourished. The Country Club Party elite participated or stood by and watched it as it all happened. That's because Pliartrum, "made them all an offer that they couldn't refuse."

The End

Made in United States
Troutdale, OR
12/23/2025

43201922R00076